THE BRIDE AND DOOM

THE BRIDE AND DOOM

ERIN SCOGGINS

HELIUM PRESS

For Sean. Always.

1

Until the day my husband ran off with my cash box and my dignity, I swore I'd never set foot in Flat Falls, North Carolina again.

But fate and my dear Aunt Beverlee had dragged me back to town on an ordinary Thursday, and instead of an afternoon spent eating cheese puffs and binging on *Gilmore Girls* reruns, I found myself climbing out of my dusty old Honda in the one town I had sworn I'd never visit again.

I kept my promise for almost ten years, steering clear of my beachfront hometown like some people dodge getting Pap smears. Ten years of carefully planned evasion.

Until today.

I swatted a fly from in front of my face and glanced down at the address I'd scribbled on the back of a Chinese take-out menu when Beverlee called in a panic that morning.

I had debated answering, knowing Beverlee would turn inside out if she knew how my life was really going. But guilt was a powerful persuader. If I didn't pick up, she would keep hitting redial until she wore me down. Or worse, she would fire up her convertible and drive the three hours to Raleigh to check on me herself. Hell hath no fury like a Southern woman who thinks she is being ignored.

"Did I wake you, Glory Ann?" she had asked, her voice thick and slow, like pancake syrup. "I'm never sure how early it's acceptable to call. You're likely to have been up late networking at one of your fancy shindigs."

I grimaced. If she meant sitting at home alone, eating cream-filled donuts from a box and watching reality television, my life was one big fancy party these days.

Beverlee filled me in on all the happenings in Flat Falls as if it hadn't been almost a decade since I rode the bus out of town with fifty dollars in birthday money, my diploma, and a suitcase stuffed with romantic, big city dreams.

She chattered for ten minutes about the conch shell she discovered on her morning beach stroll, the end of tourist season, and the success of her new spicy clam fritter recipe, while I issued noncommittal conversational noises and hunted for the remote buried beneath the cushions of the sofa that was doing double duty as my bed.

I suppressed a groan. "Can I call you back later, Beverlee?" I fished out a quarter wedged against a spring and held it up in triumph. Every bit helped these days. "I'm in the middle of something."

"Well, it won't take long. I haven't talked to you in ages, and there's so much I need to tell you," she drawled. "Life is short, baby, and it's important to reconnect with you in my old age." She paused, and her slow inhalation echoed through the phone. "You're the only family I have left."

When Beverlee pulled out the guilt card, the conversation always shifted into overtime. I plopped down on the sofa and rested my head against the cushion with a resigned sigh. "It's always nice to hear from you," I said, rubbing the bridge of my nose.

She paused, then released another deep, shaky breath.

When she finally replied, her voice was soft and tentative. "I know you're busy, but I was hoping…"

Beverlee was never tentative, so I leaned forward, a sudden rush of concern quickening my pulse. "What's going on, Beverlee?"

Then she dropped the bombshell. "Something has happened, baby. Something serious. I need you to come home. Today."

Which is how I'd ended up here, tapping my foot against a road made of crushed-up oyster shells in an empty lot, waiting for Beverlee to deliver her terrible news in person.

Gnarled live oak trees stretched their depressed branches over a clearing at the end of the deserted waterfront street. The only structures around were a rusty dumpster and a tilted, rotting pier leading across the water to a beat-up wooden boat that sat lopsided in the inlet's waves.

I remembered the large boat from my childhood, and it was dirty and unkempt even then. It was the nautical equivalent of a haunted house—worn, creaky, and laced with shadows. It had belonged to Old Bill Judson, a strange fossil of a man who hung out at the marina in the far end of town, well beyond the high-dollar tourist area. I wondered why my aunt, a sunny and exuberant member of the finer side of Flat Falls society, picked this place for our reunion.

I rummaged through my purse for my phone, found it crammed beneath a roll of duct tape and an apple, and held it in front of me to text Beverlee. No signal. Of course.

Flat Falls was a lot of things, but a beacon of technological advancement, it was not.

When the crunch of car tires on gravel approached, I turned to see a bright yellow convertible slow to a stop beside me. I was in the right spot, after all.

The door flung open, and Beverlee jumped out and dashed toward me. Dressed in hot pink from head to toe, she looked like a well-coiffed flamingo had been stuffed into a sausage casing. Her cheeks were flushed, and in her ill-advised capri pants and matching tank top, she seemed as vibrant and full of life as she always had.

Relief washed over me. Despite her ominous call earlier, she didn't look like death was standing on her front porch, waiting to escort her to the beauty parlor in the sky.

"Oh, my baby is here," she squealed, gathering me in a tight hug. She smelled like cookies, and a vanilla-scented pang of homesickness wrapped around me with a grip as tight as her arms.

After squeezing me for over a minute, she pushed me to arm's length. "Let me get a peek at you."

I tried to avoid squirming as she ran her gaze down the front of my wrinkled dress.

"Oh, you skinny thing. I'll need to step up my cooking game now that you're home."

Beverlee's love language was hospitality, and she likely had plates of her legendary Southern cooking already crowding the refrigerator in anticipation of my arrival, even though it had only been six hours since I agreed to make the trip.

I stepped back and pointed at her smooth skin and heavily made-up eyes, which shimmered in shades of lavender and silver. "You don't look sick, Beverlee."

She tilted her head, her shiny white bob bouncing. "Sick? I'm as healthy as a bucket full of kale. What makes you think I'm sick?"

I exhaled. "You called me this morning, remember? You said something had happened."

"Mmm hmmm."

"You said it was serious."

She laughed and gave a dismissive wave. "Oh, it is serious. But not bad serious."

"Beverlee," I warned, my fingernails digging into the palms of my closed fists. "Can you please tell me what's going on?"

The sound of a car driving up the street kept her from answering.

Beverlee frowned at her watch. "Hateful woman. Why can't she be fashionably late like the rest of us?"

The hospitality gene skipped over me, but the nosy one latched onto me early on. I craned my neck to get a look at the driver behind the light-colored sedan's tinted windows. "Who is—"

Beverlee crossed her arms in front of her chest and shook her head. She appeared to be counting under her breath. After a few long seconds, she nodded once, pasted a smile on her face, and pivoted toward the recent arrival.

The car door opened, and a thin, older woman climbed out. She was dressed in a beige pantsuit with cream patent pumps, her eyes obscured behind champagne-colored plastic glasses. Her sandy hair, combed back in a taut bun, continued the neutral theme. She looked like a human coffee stirrer.

She stepped forward toward Beverlee. "Good afternoon," she said, her voice crisp. "And who is our guest this afternoon?"

She scrutinized me like she was investigating a stain on the rug, her nose wrinkled and a stern line slicing down the center of her forehead. Being in Flat Falls had always made me feel that way—like an outsider who never quite fit in.

I debated pushing her into the nearby water, but at the last minute tried the high road. I reached out my hand and forced a pleasant smile. "Glory Wells. I'm Beverlee's niece."

Instead of shaking my outstretched hand, she wriggled out of her anemic jacket and laid it over my arm, then turned back to Beverlee.

Beverlee sighed, then plucked the jacket off my arm and tossed it on the trunk of the woman's car. I watched as it slid down the slick metal and puddled in the dirt. "Glory, I'd like you to meet Doris Sadler, my wedding planner."

I gaped at the two women, and a harsh bark of laughter escaped from my open mouth. "Your... what?"

Beverlee extended her left hand to display a flashy diamond, her grin wide. "I'm getting married."

I rocked back on my heels. "But I thought you were sick."

"Lovesick, maybe," she said, clasping her hands in front of her chest. "The best kind."

I mustered a feeble attempt at a smile, wanting to be excited for her, but Beverlee Wells-Bartholomew was no stranger to wedded bliss. This would be her fourth wedding, a fact I couldn't bring up without raining on her otherwise sunny demeanor. "But... who?"

She smoothed her hand down my arm. "Honey, I'm sure it seems sudden. I've always needed my space, and I had given up hope on ever finding someone to love. But then I met Edwin, and when you know, you know. Am I right?"

I thought back to my own wedding and the weeks leading up to it. Despite everybody mentioning we were rushing it and gossiping about whether there was a ticking clock hidden under my empire-waisted dress, I had been excited to become Mrs. Cobb Mulvaney. "I get it." I sighed. "But why didn't you tell me you were seeing somebody?"

She ducked her head. "You've been so busy getting back on your feet, and Lord knows I understand the value of a good wallow. But with the wedding coming up so soon, I had to force the issue." She raised her chin and met my stare. "And you would know him, too, if you came around here more often."

Let the broken record show we made it approximately

fifteen minutes before the guilt trip started. "I'm here now, Beverlee."

She clapped in excitement, the stack of thin metal bracelets on her wrist jangling like merry bells. "Yes, you are, baby. And we have so much to do before the wedding."

Doris cleared her throat and fastened an annoyed glare on Beverlee. "Now that you have wasted my time on your little family meeting, we are even further behind schedule. And if you will remember, in our earlier meetings, you led me to believe you had no family to help you plan the wedding. This is an unexpected complication."

Guilt sank into my chest. Beverlee thought she would have to do this alone. I inched back over to her side.

Beverlee looped her arm around my shoulder and drew me close. "I raised Glory like my daughter. I'm sure you've heard she's a successful event planner up in the city. And now that she's here, you'll welcome her ideas."

I pressed my palm to my mouth as yet another wave of remorse rolled through my body. Beverlee had stood up for me, no matter what kind of trouble I found myself in, for as long as I could remember. I leaned over and whispered, "Beverlee, I appreciate it, but—"

Beverlee shot me a warning stare and pulled away. She grabbed a notebook from her tote bag. "Shall we get started? The wedding is in two weeks." She held up two fingers and pointed toward the dock. "Two. Where do we stand on the boat?"

Doris eyed me for a moment, her face pinched tight, before responding. "I have spoken with Mr. Judson. He doesn't wish to have a bunch of uppity mainlanders on his property." Her lips pursed. "And that is a direct quote."

My mouth dropped open as realization hit. I whirled toward the boat. "You want to get married here? On Old Bill Judson's boat?"

7

Beverlee's gaze softened. "Did I forget to mention Edwin and I are tying the knot on the high seas?"

"You're what?" I asked in confusion.

Doris snickered, her body rigid. "Pirates. They want to dress like pirates."

Seaside weddings were the norm around Flat Falls, and I had attended more than my fair share of yacht-based nuptials, but something told me Beverlee wasn't going for nautical glamour. There wouldn't be any tasteful anchor monograms or seashell wine stoppers in my future.

I glanced around the empty lot for a hidden camera, sure this was a joke. But Beverlee was grinning, and Doris was grimacing. "You're having a themed wedding?"

Beverlee waved her hand around in front of her and faced the open water. "Imagine the colors, the fabrics, the romance."

"The humiliation," Doris muttered with an exaggerated wince.

Beverlee ignored Doris's jab and gave my shoulder a quick squeeze. "I'm sure you have some suggestions you can share with Doris."

My mind went blank. I had planned a pirate-themed birthday party for the son of a CEO once, but it involved a bouncy house and a costumed Captain Hook. And the guest of honor was six.

None of that would help me pull off a wedding for a grown woman on a boat that was minutes away from sinking to the bottom of the Intracoastal Waterway. Captains and buccaneers had been drowning here for years, but I somehow doubted that Beverlee wanted her wedding site to also be her eternal resting place.

"Doris, I'd love to discuss your plans," I said with a slight smirk. "A pirate wedding sounds… challenging."

Doris crossed her arms and spoke slowly, sarcasm dripping like melted honey between each sentence. "Weddings by the Sea prides itself on meeting the needs of our discerning customers. Most of them," she added, shooting a pointed glance toward Beverlee, "put a great deal of thought into planning graceful and timeless ceremonies."

"Of course," I said, glancing at Beverlee, who rolled her eyes.

Doris's voice rose. "Beverlee and Edwin have decided to buck the trend."

"What's more timeless than pirates?" Beverlee huffed, folding her arms across her chest.

Doris turned toward me, her pale face cracking like dried bread dough. "I'm trying to keep things classy."

Unlike my mother, a good girl to the tips of her pastel-painted toes, Beverlee lived life on her terms. Terms that usually involved a lot of color and far too many accessories. And sometimes farm animals. But she had put her entire world on hold for me without a second thought, and I couldn't let Doris continue the snide comments without defending my aunt. It was one thing for me to make fun of Beverlee, but quite another for somebody else to do it, especially when Beverlee was paying the woman.

I tilted my head toward Doris. "Isn't it your job to make the bride's dreams a reality? If she wanted to get married in a hot-air balloon dressed like Little Bo-Peep, wouldn't it be up to you to make it happen?"

Doris glared.

Beverlee beamed.

"I'm not sure you understand, Ms. Wells," Doris said, speaking to me in the same tone someone would use with a kindergartener who dared to have a potty accident on the floor. "She is getting married in two weeks, and we haven't secured a location for the ceremony. The venue the bride has chosen might sink at any moment, and the owner hasn't even agreed to let us use it."

I glanced at the boat, then leaned in toward Beverlee and lowered my voice. "I'm with her, Bev. Let's find you a pleasant spot on the beach. We'll throw out a few fishing nets and some glittery buoys for ambiance. We can even hoist a Jolly Roger. How does that sound?"

Beverlee jerked away from me. "We will get married on that boat." She pointed at Doris. "And if we don't, you won't get paid."

Doris sighed, then marched toward the pier, her beige shoes crunching against the shells in a staccato beat. "Fine. Let's get this over with."

Beverlee clapped twice, then followed Doris down the dock. "Excellent. It's a beautiful day to plan a wedding."

I surveyed the boat as I trailed Beverlee and Doris toward the water. The green wooden hull was so dark it appeared almost black. Twin masts stretched toward the sky, anchoring worn curls of rope and wire. Ornate swirls of rich wood and weathered brass lined the deck, and if I squinted just right, I could almost picture it being home to a lace-covered trellis fit for a wedding.

But that's where the romance ended. A rough carving of a mermaid served as the masthead on the front of the boat. She was missing a lot of paint and most of one breast. The pirate life hadn't been kind to her.

Her hollow black gaze followed me as I made my way down the rickety dock. I gave her an apologetic wave before I climbed aboard.

A closer inspection of the ship didn't help my impression. It reeked of mildew, bilgewater, and sausage from the red enamel kettle grill bolted to the deck. Wisps of frayed canvas slapped against the boom, and the once regal sails were lumped and knotted in awkward mounds along the wooden mast.

I approached the two women standing on the other side of the boat. "Where's our host?"

Beverlee shrugged. "Knowing Bill, he's knee-deep in his fourth beer by now."

"He doesn't know you're here, does he? How will you convince him to let you get married here if he won't even talk to you?"

She leaned forward and adjusted her tank top to display a generous amount of cleavage. "Don't you worry about that," she said. "I have my ways."

With a shudder, I changed the subject and gestured to the flat open space along the back of the boat. "That's where you want to set up for the ceremony?"

"Exactly," she said, and then pointed toward the oyster shell lot. "And since the boat isn't big enough for all of our guests, we'll set up tents with seating over there so everybody can get a good view."

I pressed my fingers into my temples to stave off the oncoming headache. "How many guests are we talking here, Beverlee?"

She flipped through a few pages of her notebook. "About a hundred, give or take," she replied.

Doris looked like she was about to be sick.

At the moment, I couldn't blame her. Beverlee had a lot of friends and considered herself a celebrity in Flat Falls. She'd never limit herself to a hundred guests. She'd be lucky to keep it to double that, and that was only if she excluded people she'd shared harsh words with over the years. Because she was a Southern woman with a decidedly Southern attitude, that number could easily amount to half the town.

I started toward the bow to get a better view of the space behind the cabin, but my foot caught on a hatch door and I tumbled forward. My purse hit the wood with a loud thud, scattering its contents along the deck floor. I muttered a potent curse as my favorite lip balm rolled away in slow motion, then disappeared over the side of the boat.

Doris bent to retrieve a granola bar that had landed on top of her shoe. She dangled it from the tips of her fingers like a dead flounder. "I think we're done here," she said, her face pinched with disgust.

2

After I retrieved the errant contents of my pocketbook, we walked back out to our cars. I told Beverlee I'd meet her at home after I ran some errands, but I actually wanted to reintroduce myself to Flat Falls without the well-meaning help of my doting aunt.

It was only a few blocks from Bill's boat to the town's waterfront, but I drove slowly, soaking in the memories of each place I passed. My elementary school was still there, including the rock I shoved Ricky Williams into when he tried to hold my hand on our fourth grade field trip to the fire station. The movie theater where I had my first official date. The hardware store where I gagged on my first sip of whiskey and earned my first paycheck.

Even the telephone pole I rammed into when Joseph Pruitt traded a sloppy French kiss for stick-shift driving lessons was still missing the chunk Beverlee's fender took out. But it looked like the town had finally replaced the pig sculpture I rammed with a forklift and dumped in the Atlantic out of spite while the rest of my neighbors watched the Founder's Day parade with sparklers and bags of cotton candy. A new bronze statue sat perched atop a stone platform in the center of downtown, flanked by spotlights and the American flag.

The pig, affectionately known as Big River Earl, stood as a monument to a Prohibition-era turf war with a neighboring town. Things got ugly when a moonshiner from across the bridge set his rival's vehicle on fire during a bootlegger roadblock. The flames missed the whiskey but barbecued the mayor's hog.

One hundred years later, and the residents of Flat Falls still held a grudge.

My daddy came from Big River, so I knew their rancor firsthand. He had never been fit for my mother, they said. A bad influence. The worst kind of scum.

The upstanding citizens of Flat Falls didn't let either of them forget he was from the wrong side of the bridge. As their only child, I wasn't allowed to forget it, either.

I carried his last name with me throughout early childhood, feeling the sting of shame when teachers called me "that Boyd girl." But after the folks from Big River claimed his body and declared they didn't want me, Beverlee packed me and my teddy bear up in her shiny red Mustang and headed to court to turn me into a Wells.

"It will be easier for you," she said, like there was anything easy about growing up as the only child of a big-hearted villain with a booming laugh, a man who liked to dance with me in the kitchen and eat chocolate ice cream straight from the carton.

By the time I passed the cemetery where my mother was buried and eased my car to a creaking stop at the water's edge, nostalgia had settled deep in my belly, tugging at my emotions.

I sat on one of the wooden swings along the causeway and stared at the water, letting memories cascade over me while the sun dropped low and the sky lit up in bright swirls of red and orange.

I left Flat Falls because small towns have long memories, and there was no way to outrun the behavior of an angry, abandoned teenager without leaving the coast altogether. Nobody forgets the wild child, and stories of my escapades had far outpaced the reality years ago. I couldn't stay in the place where my parents died, the place where I struggled to find my footing and failed again and again.

When I left, I imagined that if I ever had to come back to Flat Falls, I would be a changed woman, with a handsome husband and a successful business, maybe with a few dark-haired kids in tow.

I was going to be somebody. Somebody important. And then all the whispers about me and my parents would be meaningless.

I felt an invisible punch to the chest. Sharp, like the hand of time had reached in and wrapped her gnarled fingers around my lungs.

My breath stuttered as a breeze swept over the water. I didn't get to come back to Flat Falls a different person. Instead, I had proved them all right. I was broke and alone, and I had messed up my big life just like everybody thought I would.

I don't know how many minutes passed while I huddled on the swing, living in the tentative space between past and present. But the loud cry of a seagull snapped me back to the moment. I swallowed against the thickness in my throat, and I fumbled through my purse to check the time. Beverlee would worry if I stayed gone too long.

As I dug through my bag, though, I realized my phone wasn't there. I retraced my steps back to the car, but even after searching the floorboards and the area between the seats, I still didn't find it.

I groaned. It must have fallen out when I tripped on the boat. After beating my head against the headrest twice, I started the trip back to Old Bill's.

When I arrived, I was surprised to see Beverlee's convertible parked near the dock. I glanced around but didn't see her.

"Beverlee," I called, taking careful steps across the bumpy lot. No response.

I wondered if she had gotten a ride home with the wedding planner because she had car trouble.

I trudged down the pier toward the dilapidated boat and fought a shiver. Why would Beverlee and Edwin want to use this wreck for their ceremony?

Beverlee wanted an authentic pirate ship, but this one was battered and creepy. No lights were shining onboard or on the nearby dock. The wind picked up, slapping frayed canvas against wood as a storm brewed in the distance.

Resigned to spend as little time as possible searching for my phone, I reached for the rope line and pulled it toward me. When it creaked to a stop against the shadowy pier, I climbed aboard.

I carefully stepped toward the bow, glad I had on sturdy sandals to maneuver because the boat's deck was gritty and uneven. Not the place I would choose for my happily ever after.

I took a moment to appreciate brides who selected beautiful stone churches or tent-covered fields of wildflowers as their wedding venues. Places pre-wired for twinkle lights. Places with plumbing. Places without the rustic stench of rotting wood.

A gust of wind caused the dock lines to groan, and I steadied myself on the boom. The movement caused a nearby metal winch to shake loose and hit the wooden planks below with a loud clang. I cried out as a surge of adrenaline raced through my body, leaving me breathless and agitated.

Then, across the deck, I spotted my phone case peeking out from underneath a pile of old rags.

Just as I'd stumbled over to grab it, the wind picked up again and the boat rocked sharply. When I stooped down and closed my hand around the case, I lost my footing and landed hard, a quick jab of pain slicing through my knee. I pushed up with a curse.

I tried to steady myself on the mast, the closest thing I could find. But instead of the rough rasp of canvas I expected, my hand wrapped around something smooth and cool.

I parted the folds of canvas with shaking fingers. A jolt of panic shot through me, and my vision swirled. I was not holding onto a piece of the boat. Instead, I had a firm grasp on the cream-colored pump of Doris Sadler, the town's resident wedding planner, who was dangling from the mast like she had been hoisted up there by Blackbeard himself.

Her eyes were wide open and accusing, but her perfect beige pantsuit still seemed crisp and polished against the boat's splintering exterior.

Just then, my aunt's heels echoed on the dock. "Yoo-hoo, Glory!" She shouted in a singsong voice. "What are you doing back here, baby? I thought we were meeting at home."

I stepped back to the side of the boat but couldn't bring myself to respond. This was the first time I had ever seen a dead body that hadn't been dressed up and arranged by a mortician, and I wasn't sure how to announce it. "Um, Beverlee?"

Beverlee didn't stop her chatter as she came into view. "Well, isn't this so romantic at sunset? I can see it now, Edwin in his finest ruffled shirt and me as his pirate wench. It's perfect. I can't understand why Doris was so against this as an option. She said it would be tacky. Can you imagine? That woman having a say on what's tacky? It's like she invented the word." She traced her hand down the side of the boat in a slow caress. "I wonder if Old Bill will let us have our honeymoon on board."

I swallowed against the bile rising in my throat. "Beverlee," I said, my voice raw.

"Oh, just look at this wood. I'll bet she was quite a beauty in her time."

"Beverlee!" I tried with more force.

She came up behind me. "What, sweetheart? No need to shout. I'm right here."

I pointed toward the third guest on the boat, who was swaying in the sea breeze above our heads between the folds of the worn ivory sail. "We have a problem."

Beverlee looked up at the body, her bright red mouth going round as she gasped. "Oh my," she whispered. "Well, that explains why she didn't return my text earlier."

It did not explain, however, how Doris Sadler had ended up hoisted into the air by her neck on the very boat Beverlee had chosen to host her pirate I do's.

When the police arrived a few minutes later in response to my frantic 911 call, darkness wrapped around the scene like a shawl. The first thing they saw was my aunt, who had parked herself on the edge of the dock with her shoulders slumped and her bare feet drooping toward the water.

I paced back and forth, still wondering how I had gone from sitting on my sofa with peace and quiet and a pint of Ben & Jerry's to standing on a dock in my hometown a mere fifteen feet away from a dangling dead human, when a bright flashlight beam swept across my face. "Well, I'll be. Glory Wells, is that you? Didn't think I'd be seeing you around here anytime soon."

My vision had adjusted to the darkness enough that, with

the help of the flashlight now pointing at the ground, I could make out the Flat Falls Police Chief, Hollis Goodnight. He didn't look much different from the last time I saw him, except for a few more wrinkles on his sun-weathered face and a patch of gray hairs standing at attention on the top of his head. He always looked like he had been running his fingers through his hair, but as a teenager I thought it was from being exasperated at me. Now, though, it appeared he was always exasperated. I attempted a nervous smile. "Hi, Chief Goodnight. Long time, no see."

He engulfed me in a tight hug. His familiar scent, half leather and half coffee beans, comforted me, and I resisted the urge to ask if he would just stand there and hold me until my nerves calmed down. He had been a fixture around the outskirts of my life since I was a child, and it surprised me how much I'd missed him.

He planted a quick kiss on the top of my head. "You're old enough to call me Hollis now, I suppose. So, what's this I hear about a body on Old Bill's boat? You sure you didn't just see a sail bag? It's mighty dark out here, it could have been anything, and you haven't been around boats in a while."

He laughed, and with a sigh, I pointed toward the mast. He shined his flashlight up and the beam landed on the body, now rocking back and forth with the boat's motion on the water. "What in the world?" His expression hardened. "What have you gotten yourself into this time, Glory?"

My cheeks burned, the same way they always did when Hollis caught me doing something I wasn't supposed to be doing. Like when he caught me under the bleachers kissing a football player or found me on the beach drinking pink lemonade wine coolers instead of sitting in tenth-grade geometry class. This time I had done nothing, though. This time it wasn't my fault. "We found her like that. I didn't do it."

He nodded, his brows furrowed in concentration. "I'm sure you didn't. But we need to have a chat about what you were doing here, anyway."

Just then, Beverlee stepped up to join the conversation. She swatted him on the arm. "Hollis, leave her alone. She just got back into town this afternoon. She hasn't been home long enough to get into trouble."

I felt the low sting of shame and remembered why I had left Flat Falls to begin with. No matter how old I got, people were still expecting me to screw up.

Hollis focused on Beverlee, a flush climbing his cheeks. He had been looking at her like that since I was a kid, and I don't think she had ever noticed. "I hear congratulations are in order." He didn't offer his well-wishes, and instead picked at an invisible piece of lint on the front of his uniform. "Eddie's a lucky man. I still need to know what you're doing here this late."

I peeked down at my phone. It was a little after nine.

Beverlee sighed. "Bill texted me and asked me to meet him here to talk about using the boat for my upcoming event. But when I got here, I couldn't find him."

"Is that what we're calling it now? An event?" He grunted and climbed on board the boat. "You always knew how to throw an excellent party, Beverlee. But this is the first time one of your shindigs has involved a murder."

3

_____

After we gave our statements to Hollis and his detective, an attractive blond guy named Gage from my high school, we sat on the dock and watched the police team pull Doris down from the mast. They cranked the winch, and it made a dull scraping sound as her body dropped a few inches at a time. After they lowered her to the deck, they released the rope from around her neck, leaving her in a jumbled heap on the weathered teak surface.

Until they covered her body with a mildewed green tarp, I couldn't stop gawking at her face. Her eyes were still open and riveted right on me. I wasn't sure if dead bodies always glared, but it made me uncomfortable to be near her.

"What an interesting night," Beverlee said, leaning in with a conspiratorial whisper. "Can't say she didn't have it coming, though."

I swung around to make sure nobody heard her. "Beverlee, you can't go around saying things like that."

"Well, why not?" she asked, her penciled-in eyebrows rising toward her hairline. "Everybody around here had a beef with Doris Sadler. She was about the meanest woman I've ever met."

Squeezing my eyes closed, I shushed her again. "I don't understand why you would hire her to plan your wedding, then," I whispered.

Beverlee smirked, then stood and brushed off the seat of her bright pink pants, now streaked with a thin layer of dirt and grit from the dock. "Just because she was a mean old snake doesn't mean she didn't know how to throw a fantastic party. Remember that *Lord of the Rings*-themed barbecue I told you about? The one with the full-sized hobbit house built out of sand next to Town Hall? That was Doris. Or the disco fundraiser for the children's hospital with John Travolta as the emcee? People yammered about that party for ages. Don't you think my wedding deserves the same level of attention?"

Like generations of smart-aleck Southern women before her, Beverlee used humor to deflect attention away from her emotions. I could tell Doris's death had shaken her, but there was no way she'd admit it in front of mixed company.

Instead, her hands silently quivered as she pulled me to a stand next to her. "That's enough talk. You must be exhausted from traveling all day, not to mention the shock of everything that's happened this evening. Let's get you in bed. We need to plan a wedding, starting first thing tomorrow morning."

I followed Beverlee's convertible to the bungalow I had called home since I was a newly orphaned six-year-old, sullen and devastated after my parents died during a date night car ride along the coast. It turns out joyrides aren't so joyful when you get T-boned by a semi.

Beverlee's cottage sat on a charming, tree-lined street a few blocks from the water, and, from the looks of it, remained untouched in the years I was gone.

The motion sensor front porch light flickered on, high-lighting a wind chime made of turquoise sea glass and silver chips that still tinkled from the worn tin awning out front. Two weathered red rocking chairs sat side by side on the front porch, flanked by a three-foot-tall chicken sculpture. The rainbow-striped sign I painted for her in middle school that said Welcome to the Beach had faded over time, but still hung next to the front door.

From the sunny yellow siding to the bright teal shutters and flower boxes bursting with colorful plants, Beverlee's home had always been vibrant and welcoming, much like the woman who called it home for the past twenty-five years.

Her keys jangled as she pushed open the door. She tossed them on the counter and flicked the light switch, bathing the kitchen in a warm golden glow.

I had always loved her kitchen, and aside from a few appliance upgrades and some shiny new cooking gadgets, it still looked the same.

My eyes stung as I brushed my hand along the worn oak table that still stood as the room's centerpiece. Many of my most important moments happened around its edges. I had cried here, laughed here, and been lectured and loved here. "You look hungry," Beverlee said quietly, already moving toward the refrigerator.

My stomach lurched at the thought of eating, but telling Beverlee you didn't want to eat her food was like confessing you were an ax murderer or an introvert. Either way, she would stuff you full and hope that her tray of pickled peaches and garden-fresh green beans was enough to make you see the light.

I rested my hand on my stomach. "Maybe in a few minutes."

She stared at me for a moment, then nodded and

grabbed the worn-out suitcase from my hand before heading off down the hall toward my childhood bedroom.

Before I left, I said I'd visit often, but aside from her coming to Raleigh for quick weekend visits, we just stayed in touch through regular phone calls and Facebook posts. With the low hum of guilt as background noise, I followed behind her, not sure how to make up for all the time that had passed.

I paused in the living room and smiled at the collection of rescued goods she picked up at flea markets and estate sales over the years. Whether it was an old typewriter missing its space bar or a woodland statue with the gnome's nose chopped off, Beverlee had always been a guardian of lost and broken things.

That included me.

Beverlee had been the mother in my life since I was a child, and it was her face I pictured in most of my family memories. She had held me when I cried, made up outrageous dirty lyrics to popular songs instead of singing boring lullabies, and taught me how to hot-wire her second husband's prized junker while most of my friends were at ballet class.

"I've got a few work things spread out in your old room, but it won't be any trouble to get it ready for you," Beverlee said as I joined her in my former bedroom.

Once plastered with boy band posters and rainbow pillows, the room had been converted into a small office. The old pine desk where I'd avoided doing homework was a computer workstation with two large monitors attached to a high-dollar laptop. My ruffled purple bed had been shoved into the corner, now covered with photography equipment.

Beverlee pointed at the bed, where several colored printouts were laid out. "Did I tell you I've been working on a new fancy foods line? It has been such fun. Edwin thinks I'll be able to sell it to all the ritzy specialty food shops in the area because everybody loves a home-cooked meal. He thinks I'll be the next Paula Deen."

A flicker of sadness sparked inside me. I knew my room wasn't a shrine, untouched in my absence. But I was still taken aback with the confirmation that there was nowhere left where I truly belonged.

Beverlee busied herself with pulling out blankets and pillows and positioning a glass of water on the nightstand as she'd done at bedtime since I was a kindergartener.

The routine was a comforting reminder of my childhood, and I wondered if I was wrong to have stayed away for so long. Then she handed me a pair of bright orange construction earplugs. Because Edwin might be visiting later, she said the earplugs might help me sleep better.

The night ended with me tired, but wired, and staring at the glow-in-the-dark stars I stuck to the ceiling when I was twelve because I was still scared of the dark and it seemed more mature than begging for a night light. When headlights flashed against my window and I heard two people walking down the hall toward Beverlee's bedroom, I wished there was a way for me to erase almost everything I'd experienced that day.

Sleep, when it finally came, was fitful and dotted with dreams of a sixty-something beige woman, swinging from a rope and staring at me with a cold, colorless glare.

I woke the next morning to the aroma of coffee and bacon, and I stumbled into the kitchen expecting to find Beverlee in front of the stove like she always was, her hair wrapped in a bright scarf and a fresh coat of makeup already applied. But Beverlee wasn't there. Instead, a sturdy, white-haired man sat at the kitchen table, a full mug and the morning newspaper spread out in front of him.

He wasn't a small man, but he looked even larger wrapped in Beverlee's light pink fuzzy robe. He had the leathery, sun-worn skin of a fisherman, with wiry white hairs and a small anchor tattoo on his chest. The sides of the robe didn't meet in the middle and I was eternally grateful that the most important bits were hidden beneath the table.

He started to rise when I entered the kitchen. "No!" I screeched and averted my gaze to avoid an embarrassing early morning introduction that I couldn't recover from, revealing more of my future uncle than I needed to see before I was fully awake. "Don't get up."

His eyes widened. "Not a morning person, I take it?" He nodded toward the hallway. "Neither is your aunt. You come by it honestly."

He smiled and extended his hand. "I'm Edwin Calhoun, and you must be Glory, the prodigal niece. I'm sorry to hear you had such a scare last night. How are you holding up?"

I shook his hand and shuffled to the cabinet for a mug, closing my eyes against the image of Doris that flashed through my memory. "I've had better nights."

"It must have been horrible. I can't even imagine." He leaned back in his chair. "Well, I'm glad to have this chance to get to know you better. Beverlee has told me so much about you, but meeting you in person has added another layer to the stories."

I snorted. If there was one thing I knew, it was that my aunt had an arsenal of fish tales about me. Some of them were even true.

"She's proud of you, Glory, and tickled to pieces you're home." He smiled, his kind gray eyes crinkling at the edges. I could understand why Beverlee liked him so much. He met my eyes when he spoke, which was already a few steps ahead of boob-staring husband number three.

I poured a cup of coffee, plucked a crisp piece of bacon from Beverlee's favorite stoneware platter, and leaned against the counter. "It's nice to see her so happy."

"I'm the lucky one," he said with a soft chuckle. "After my first wife died, I didn't think I'd be fortunate enough to find love again. She might be wild and unusual, but your aunt is the best thing that has happened to me in a very long time."

His gaze dropped to my hand, where I was absently twirling my wedding ring around my finger. Despite being without a husband for over six months, I hadn't taken the ring off.

That would have to change. I would need the money more than I needed the diamond before too long.

"Beverlee told me about the troubles you had with your husband," he said gently. "I'm sorry to hear about your struggles."

I shrugged and wiggled the ring off my finger. "I was thinking about taking it down to the pawnshop later today."

He leaned forward and held out his hand. "May I?"

"Sure." I dropped the ring into his outstretched palm.

He raised it to the light, examining the stone before handing it back to me. "I wish I could tell you what to ask for it, but I'm afraid jewelry isn't my thing." He lowered his voice and glanced toward the hallway. "But don't tell Beverlee that. She thinks it's romantic that I let her pick out her ring."

I smiled. "She was showing it off last night. It's beautiful."

"She convinced me she needed a big rock to symbolize our big love." He chuckled. "And I've been around long enough to never stand between a woman and her jewelry fantasies."

He rested his palm on the top of my hand, his calloused fingertips both scratchy and comforting. "I don't want to sound presumptuous," he said. "But it might be time for you and your snazzy ring to get a fresh start."

A swirl of shame tumbled through me and I shifted in my chair, dropping the ring into the zippered change pocket in my wallet.

"We're here to help you, Glory," he said gently. "Because that's what family does. All you have to do is ask."

Edwin's concerned expression turned soft as Beverlee sashayed into the kitchen and dropped onto a chair with a dramatic groan. Her normally well-styled silver hair was askew, and the remnants of last night's lipstick still outlined the edges of her mouth. It looked like the love fest had gone on well into the morning. Ew.

Edwin rose to fix her a cup of coffee and I let out a sigh of relief at the flash of denim shorts peeking out from under my aunt's robe.

She sipped the coffee he offered, and her eyes fluttered closed as she inhaled. Her hands cradled the cup. "Just the way I like it."

Edwin planted a kiss on the top of her head and turned to wink at me. "I aim to please, ladies."

Beverlee reached up to rest her hand on his scruffy cheek. "Yes. Yes, you do."

"So, how did you two lovebirds meet?" I asked.

Edwin rested against the counter. "It was serendipity at its finest. I was minding my own business at the fish market one day when this beautiful woman came in and bought all of my lionfish."

Beverlee lifted a shoulder, the hint of a smile visible over the mug she held close to her mouth. "I had a new recipe. Lionfish are hard to find around here."

Edwin rested a hand on her shoulder. "We talked about

food and Flat Falls and how I was new in town." He paused and gave her a gentle squeeze, then let his hand linger, his thumb caressing her collarbone. "So, there I was, tripping over my tongue because she was beautiful and smart and unusual. I was smitten from the start."

I could believe it. My aunt was a standout in every way. Loud, eccentric, and unaware of both, she was a Southerner down to sweet-tea-soaked bones. She had always welcomed people into her home with a chilled glass of lemonade or a plate of fresh butterscotch cookies, and she didn't let them leave until she had showered them with advice and learned all their secrets. Over-the-top hospitality was her gift to the world.

"I thought he was handsome, and you know I love to feed a hungry man." She tossed her hair. "So, I invited him to dinner."

"And I never left. Your aunt is an amazing woman, Glory, and it appears to run in your family." He thumped his fist over his heart. "I promise to love and cherish you both."

Beverlee rested her hand over his, a gesture so sweet and pure it was hard to swallow past the lump in my throat. A quick snap of jealousy blurred my vision. I wanted someone to love me like that.

Edwin took one last sip of his coffee and rinsed out his mug. "I'm going to go get prettied up. Do you girls have big plans for the day?"

I shrugged. "Wedding stuff, I suppose."

Beverlee let out a dramatic sigh and rolled her eyes. "Just like that Doris Sadler to leave me in the lurch like this. I feel bad that she's dead, but my to-do list is now a mile long."

Edwin patted her cheek. "I feel confident you two can handle it. I can't wait to hear what you dream up."

He disappeared down the hallway and reappeared a few minutes later, dressed for the day in a button-up chambray shirt and khaki linen pants. Snagging a piece of bacon off the counter, he paused only long enough to wiggle his long white brows at Beverlee before popping it into his mouth.

He leaned forward and brushed a kiss across her cheek, then passed by and put a comforting hand on my shoulder, giving it a soft squeeze before he grabbed his keys off the counter. "I'll leave you two ladies to catch up. Maybe I can come by here later for lunch."

"And dessert," Beverlee responded, a blush climbing her cheeks.

I tried not to shudder at the thought of their geriatric afternoon delight.

Edwin chuckled. "I'm looking forward to it."

He pushed the door open to walk out but stopped short. "Looks like you've got a visitor." Edwin stepped back into the kitchen, straightening his back and squaring his shoulders. Through the window, I spotted Chief Goodnight heading down the driveway.

"Morning," Edwin said, nodding once in the universal greeting males give each other when grunting would be rude.

As he approached the door, Hollis nodded once in return, and I noticed he stood taller, too. They were like peacocks, coming just short of pulling out their man bits and strutting around.

Edwin narrowed his eyes at the chief and turned to Beverlee. "I can stay if you need me, sweetheart."

Beverlee tucked her hair behind her ear. "No, no. You've got a busy day. I'll see you later."

After a moment's hesitation, Edwin gave Hollis a hard stare and elbowed past him to stride out of the cottage.

I jumped up to break the tension. "Good morning," I said, and motioned for the chief to come inside. "Can I get you a cup of coffee?"

Hollis closed the door behind him and patted his stomach. "Already had two cups this morning. Shirley wouldn't serve me anymore because she said I'm too high strung as it is, and she didn't think it was a good idea if an officer of the law had too much caffeine and got shaky with his trigger finger."

I gawked at the gun on his belt with alarm. "Are you planning on shooting somebody today?"

"Depends. Got anybody for me to shoot?"

My thoughts flew to my ex-husband. "I could probably start you a list."

He tipped his head toward me. "When I need some side action, I'll be sure to give you a call."

His definition of side action and mine were completely different.

Since he hadn't mentioned why he was there, I broached the subject. "You're an early bird this morning. Did you come with news about what happened to Doris Sadler last night?"

Hollis scrubbed his hand along the stubble on his jaw. "We have opened a full investigation and I'm trying to piece together what happened. I was hoping you two ladies would give me some information."

I flashed back to the woman's bulging eyes and my stomach clenched. "It was terrible." I grasped the back of a kitchen chair to steady myself and took a deep breath. "But we're happy to help with the investigation. What can we do?"

He landed a steely glare on Beverlee. "You can start by telling me the whole story."

I looked back and forth between my aunt and Hollis, wondering what I was missing. "I think we told you everything last night. Right, Beverlee?"

His gaze shifted across the table. "I realize you had quite a scare last night, Glory. But your aunt here seems to have left something out when she was recounting the events of last evening."

I glanced at Beverlee in confusion, then back to Hollis. "What did she leave out?"

"Word on the street is that you were the last person to see Doris Sadler alive." He lifted a finger and pointed at Beverlee. "And that the two of you were having a rather heated discussion outside the Grind and Go right before her demise."

I whipped my head around and studied my aunt, who sat at the table and sipped her coffee as if she didn't have a care in the world.

"What are you implying, Chief Goodnight?" I asked.

"I'm not implying anything, Glory. I'm trying to put everything together. And it seems like she has one giant puzzle piece she forgot to mention last night. A piece that seems to be very relevant, seeing as how this is now a murder investigation."

I stared at Beverlee, who seemed in no hurry to answer questions. When she didn't offer information, impatience rolled through me. "Well?" I huffed.

"Well, what?" She waved her hand in the air as if she were dismissing a fly. "Glory, you understand how important this day is. I want it to be unique. Special, like my love for Edwin."

I glanced up to see Hollis roll his eyes. "So, what were you fighting about?" I asked.

"We weren't fighting. I was simply telling her I expected her to treat you with more respect. I reminded her that if she didn't listen to what I wanted, I would find another wedding planner."

"There's not another wedding planner in Flat Falls, Beverlee. She was the only one. And your wedding is only two weeks away."

Beverlee gave another dismissive wave. "Right? And now she's left me in this ridiculous bind."

I gaped at her. "It's not like she chose to get strung up like a bloated mackerel on that boat."

"I know that, Glory. I'm sure if she had her choice, she'd have gotten knocked off somewhere classier."

"Ladies, I don't want to interrupt your family discussion," Hollis said, tapping the brim of his hat against the counter. "But I need to investigate where Doris went after you visited with her at the restaurant."

Beverlee let out a long, slow sigh. "Well, I don't know, Hollis. It was a tedious night. She probably climbed on her broom and went out for a bite to eat. Look for a buffet serving toad eyeballs or small children somewhere in town."

"Beverlee," he warned.

"Okay, fine," she said, defiantly crossing her arms, a move she'd probably picked up during my teenage years. "She mentioned going back by her office to get her assistant so they could put another venue proposal together for Bill. But that was about an hour before... you know." She made a sawing motion across the front of her neck before settling her hands in her lap, fingers clenched tightly together.

Hollis cleared his throat. "We're looking for someone who could have hauled the body on deck and winched it up on the mast. There's a pool down at the station that says Beverlee's too old to lift a body that high."

Beverlee's chair scraped the floor, and she rose to her feet, her hands tucked firmly on her ample hips. "Did you just call me weak?"

He stuck his palms out toward her. "I've seen you reel in a three hundred-pound bluefin tuna by yourself during a raging thunderstorm. I have no doubt you could handle Doris Sadler, which is part of the problem. You were the last person to see her alive and one of the first people at the crime scene. That looks mighty suspicious."

I dropped my head to the table with a thud.

Hollis snatched up his hat and turned toward the door but glanced over his shoulder before he twisted the knob. "Stick close to home, ladies. I'm sure I'll have more questions."

After Hollis left, I yanked a pad of paper from Beverlee's junk drawer. "I'm tired of thinking about dead people. What's our plan for the day?"

Beverlee stepped to the sliding glass door to her backyard with a plate full of vegetable scraps she had retrieved from the refrigerator. She slid the door open and a handful of chickens clucked their way up onto her deck. I recognized her favorite, a black-and-white fluff ball named Matilda, from the countless pictures she had texted me over the past year. Beverlee took chicken pictures like some people took duck-faced makeup selfies.

"I have some work to do this morning," she said, holding out a handful of carrot peels to the chickens, who were prancing and waddling around to get a bite. "I have a new blog post coming out on the edible uses for kudzu."

Right before I graduated from high school, Beverlee had become involved with husband number two, who ran the town's newspaper. As a wedding gift to his blushing bride, he gave her a cooking column in the paper. It had become a wild success, and even after the divorce, her ex-husband had named her a moneymaker and let her keep doing it.

Now Beverlee's column ran right below the fold every Tuesday, and she had her own blog. *Beverlee's Bites* focused on Southern recipes, entertaining tidbits, and chicken stories, and was basically my aunt's personal gossip rag.

"People eat kudzu? Like the kudzu that grows along the back fence?"

Beverlee tipped her head toward a bowl overflowing with purple flowers sitting on the counter. "They're delicious. They taste like grapes. I'm fixing to make some kudzu jelly if you want to stay and help. Edwin helped me design a gorgeous label covered with vines, and the ritzy gift shop over in Big River has already ordered a case for their Made in North Carolina display."

I shook my head. The last thing I wanted to do was make jelly from yard weeds. "It's great that you're selling your fence foliage, but I think I'll pass," I said, picturing the diamond ring burning a hole in my purse. "Besides, I have a few things I need to do this morning."

4

I parked in front of the pawnshop and stared up at the flashing neon sign that said I could buy, sell, or trade anything I wanted, any time I wanted. I figured the first day after finding a dead body was as good a time as any to get my life back, so I slipped the ring back onto my finger and prepared for battle.

Chin out. Shoulders down. I pushed the buzzer beside the pawnshop's metal-barred front door and waited. Within seconds, a short, sixty-something woman with purple hair peeked her head out from behind the counter. She stared at me through the window for a moment, then chuckled and hit the buzzer.

With a deep breath, I pushed the door open and stepped inside. It swung closed behind me and locked with a jarring *thunk*. I found myself surrounded by the musty scent only an old junk shop could provide, a combination of reheated Thanksgiving dinners and someone's backside. Familiar, yet not entirely pleasant.

Kind of like my life these days.

"Need something?" the woman said, her voice hoarse like

she'd downed a pint of whiskey. Given how it smelled in there, she might have.

I lifted my hand in a wave and tried to ignore the skitter of nervous energy winding through my belly. "Hey, Scoots."

She folded her arms across her chest and leaned against the counter. "Glory Wells. I thought pigs would have to be flying down the beach for you to come back here."

I ignored the familiar sting of reproach that had followed me around Flat Falls since I was a kid. "Did I say that?"

"Believe me, it was one of the nicer things you said before you left town."

Scoots was one of the old-timers around here. She knew the history of the town and every one of its residents and there wasn't a misdeed or errant comment that didn't get tucked away in her mental filing cabinet.

She stared at me for a minute, stretching out the inspection like putty. I fought the urge to fidget under her heavy gaze. After a few moments, she stepped away from the counter and reeled me in for a tight hug. Since she was so short, her face smashed into my chest and the tips of her spiky hair pressed into the flesh under my chin. When she stepped back, she flashed a saucy grin. "It's good to see you, kiddo. I don't see any airborne swine, though, so you must be here about that dead woman."

My breakfast threatened to reappear on her freshly cleaned glass display case. "Did you know her?" I asked.

Scoots dipped her chin, "Well enough, I suppose. It's a shame what happened. Nobody deserves to take their last breath on a boat that smells like stale beer and rotten barbecue. Do they have a suspect yet?"

"Hollis came by this morning asking questions," I answered. "They're working on it."

She stared at me for a long moment, then grinned. "Well, if you're not here to bring me gossip, what good are you?"

I nodded to a worn cardboard sign propped against the front window. "Are you still buying jewelry?"

"Sure. Gold, silver, platinum. What have you got?"

I twirled the ring around my finger, its weight a sensation I hadn't been without for seven years. "I need to sell my happily ever after." With a tug, I pulled it off and dropped it on the counter, listening to it spin for a few seconds before hitting the surface with a solid thud.

Scoots picked it up and brought it to her nose, squinting as she moved it under the jeweler's loupe she had on a chain around her neck. "You get into a fight? None of my business, I know. But it's rare for a pretty lady like you to come in here trying to get rid of a mountain."

My cheeks prickled with heat. "No fight."

"Then why—"

I shuffled back and forth on my feet, trying not to let my impatience show. "We're not together anymore and I… I need the money."

She nodded. "I remember hearing something about your husband trouble, now that you mention it. It was the talk of the town a while back. You always knew how to get tongues flapping around here." Her face softened, and she leaned toward me before whispering, "Tough break, but don't you have anything else you can sell?"

I picked at a thread on the front of my shirt. There wasn't anything. No more bottles of overpriced wine, no antique furniture, no fancy clothes for the gilded life of a high-profile event planner. Humiliation snaked up my spine. I didn't want to tell her the ring was all I had left.

Over the last few months, I had sold the pieces of my life with Cobb one by one. I even held a yard sale to get cash for rent. Nothing said "my life has fallen to ruin" better than seven years of chipped china and thrift store furniture, laid out for the world to see.

I sold everything down to the toilet plunger hanging on our garage wall.

But selling Cobb's things was the hardest. For a while, everything he left behind sat untouched, waiting for his return. But I finally had to accept that he wasn't coming back. So, I started selling his things, piece by piece, until his side of the closet was bare.

I even thought about hocking his underwear, but I didn't want to take the chance that his designer boxer briefs carried bad karma. It would have been tacky to charge somebody for that level of bad relationship juju.

I sighed. "Beverlee's getting married."

"I heard," she said with a coarse chuckle. "Nice guy."

I closed my eyes to avoid rolling them, then pinched the bridge of my nose. "Lucky number four. I hope he knows what he's getting into."

Scoots snorted. "That woman needs a frequent visitor card to the matrimonial aisle, doesn't she?"

I pointed to the ring on the counter. "We're big fans of love in the Wells family."

She stared at me for a moment, then picked up the ring. She tapped it on the counter a few times, her lips drawn into a grim line. "I'm sorry I don't have better news, but this isn't worth very much."

I grabbed the ring from her hand and held it up to the light. "Excuse me?"

"I'm sorry, but it looks like he slipped you a nice-looking fake."

Just like him, I thought. A nice-looking fake.

She handed me a magnifying glass and pointed at the two-carat stone sitting in the center of the gold band. "The stone has some small chipping along the facet lines. It's a dead giveaway."

It wasn't surprise that rocked me back on my heels.

Instead, anger fizzed just underneath my skin. I was angry that he left, angry that I fell for his lies, and angry that I had to return to Flat Falls with nothing more to show of my big plans than a phony diamond and another tally mark on the Glory Wells Wall of Shame that I was fairly sure existed somewhere in Flat Falls Town Hall.

Scoots seemed to sense my change in mood. She rested her hand on the counter and turned to me with a gentle smile, rare for the woman known for her surly attitude and smart-aleck comments. "Are you heading back to your aunt's house?"

I leaned down on the glass case, my head in my hands. "Please don't make me."

"Why, are you two not getting along?"

"It's not that." Raising my head, I told her about the orange earplugs and seeing a little too much of Edwin that morning. "She's happy, but she's a little too happy, if you know what I mean." I wiggled my eyebrows.

Scoots nodded and walked over to the register. She shuffled through a stack of papers, then pulled out a small cardboard square. "I might have somewhere you can stay until the wedding. That way you can give the lovebirds some much-needed privacy and keep your innocence intact."

I snorted and took the paper from her outstretched hand. But it wasn't a business card for a realtor or a hotel chain like I expected. Instead, it was an empty matchbook, the rough surface long worn off and the cardboard bent back to flat.

I flipped it over in my hand. It belonged to a restaurant I had never heard of. Trolls. 142 Water Street. "Thanks," I said. "I don't want to be in the way at Beverlee's house."

"Don't thank me yet," she replied, pointing at the card. "You'll have to get the key from Ian."

~

IAN STRICKLAND WAS the boy who got away. Or, more correctly, the man I had dumped to run off for my big life in the big city. Either way, I was pretty sure seeing me would be on his list right up next to getting a root canal or a personal visit from the IRS.

My chest tightened as I reread the matchbook I had gotten from Scoots.

Water Street was the Flat Falls beach road. Crowded with tourist shops and expensive condos, it wound its way through town and ended at a park lined with benches and the wooden swings where I had ended up the night before.

In the bright sunshine, it resembled any beach town along North Carolina's coast. Old-town charm competed with the need for swanky, upscale shops and bistros. There were shiny glass storefronts right next to worn-down bargain shops with owners who could hold out for the higher bids that would come with big-money investors.

As I walked, I passed several restaurants, but when I got to the end of the street, all I found was a henna tattoo parlor with a gold-flecked 140 painted on the door.

Confused, I double-checked the matchbook, sure I was missing something. But there were no more buildings.

I circled the building, making my way through a half-filled parking lot and down a sandy path that led toward the large bridge connecting the town to the mainland.

Remembering the times I spent as a kid running up and down this path to play under that same bridge, I smiled. I used to find so many treasures there. From washed up bottles to worn pieces of driftwood carved by the sea, it was a place of mystery and magic. It was also where I went when I missed my parents or wanted to nurse a broken heart or my wounded pride.

When I got older, that was where Ian and I met to dip our toes into adulthood. We worried about our futures and talked about our biggest secrets while listening to the cars zoom by overhead.

I rounded the corner at the end of the path, surprised that my debris-filled refuge under the bridge had been replaced by a building.

Gray-shingled walls, built into the space under the tall bridge's expanse, had taken a beating from the climate. Instead of looking dirty or worn, though, they were chic and weathered. The only decoration was a red and white life preserver ring strapped to the door. On the foam surface, written in faded black marker, it said Trolls.

Just then, the door burst open and a young man in a swimsuit and flip-flops exited. The sound of beach music and smell of fried seafood followed him out the door. He saw me and stopped short. "Sorry. Almost ran you down." He held the door open and motioned for me to go inside.

When I pushed through the door, I realized it wasn't a shack. It was a restaurant. And what the front of the building lacked in modern touches, the inside more than made up for. Massive glass doors folded open to the water, and people gathered around the worn tables, laughing and talking. The familiar scents of seawater and Old Bay filled the air.

A redheaded woman in a tank top and ponytail waved in greeting. "Hey there. Welcome to Trolls. Sit anywhere you'd like, and I'll be right with you."

"I'm… uh… looking for someone." I glanced down at the floor and then mustered up my courage to push aside the prickle of nervousness that kept my feet glued to the ground. "Ian. I'm looking for Ian."

The woman laughed. "Yeah, we'd all like a little Ian, wouldn't we?" She nodded toward the bar. "He ran to the back for a second before the lunch rush hits."

I shuffled toward the bar and ran my finger along one of the stained wooden stools. I lowered my head, my deep breath a ploy to gather another round of courage. Today was full of surprises, not the least of which was me standing in the middle of a bar waiting to ask someone who hated me if he could give me a place to stay.

"What can I get for you?" A deep voice startled me, and I jerked my head up.

I felt the jolt of familiar brown eyes. Eyes that once upon a time had crinkled when we laughed over shared jokes. Eyes that had shuttered in sadness when I walked away because I couldn't stand the idea of spending the rest of my life in the same town that had let both my parents and me down.

"Hello, Ian." My voice sounded squeaky, and I let out a small cough to cover it up.

His intense stare burned like flames against my skin.

"What are you doing here?" he demanded, his words harsh and unwelcoming, and I had the sudden urge to flee.

I backed up slowly, warmth and confusion buzzing around in my head. "Scoots said you could help me."

He cursed under his breath. "She knows better than that."

"I'm sorry, I—"

He shook his head and scrubbed at the bar with a worn white towel. "I don't have what you need."

My insides sparked with a single flash. *Oh, you definitely have what I need.*

I groaned at my traitorous body. It wasn't the time for a trip down memory lane with Ian, no matter how nice the view. And besides, once upon a time, I had chosen my freedom over him. A guy like Ian wouldn't forget that.

I held out the matchbook, my hand trembling. I shoved it back into my pocket, hoping he wouldn't see his effect on me. "Sorry. I just—"

"Again. Why are you here?" His nostrils flared, and he continued to stare without speaking.

"Vacation. Only two weeks. Beverlee's getting married, but I can't stay with them because—" I shut my mouth to stop the nervous babbling.

Ian held up his hand.

"I mean here." He jabbed the glossy bar with the tip of his finger. "Why here?"

I took a deep, hesitant breath and answered honesty. "Scoots said you have somewhere I can stay until the wedding."

"No." He flattened his palm on the bar.

"I won't be in your way, I promise. And I'm really quiet."

He raised a brow but remained silent.

"Things have changed, Ian." I sighed. "Please, I need somewhere to go."

"I said no." His voice was firm, without even a hint of its former warmth.

I swallowed. "Scoots said to remind you that you owe her one."

"Resorting to bribery now?" he asked, shaking his head. Disgust filled his tone. "I should be surprised, but I'm not."

"No," I replied softly, my shoulders slumping under his judgmental stare. "I'm just asking for help from an old friend."

His fist clenched the towel until his knuckles turned white to match it. He continued to stare, and I squirmed under the scrutiny. Finally, he reached behind the bar and whipped out a key ring. He flipped through it and found the key he wanted, then slipped it off the ring and slid it across the counter. "It's one of the apartments above the pawnshop. It belongs to Scoots, but I help her with the upkeep. Two weeks, that's it. Don't wreck the place."

I thought about the alternative and realized I didn't have much of a choice. I took the key. "Deal."

~

I TOOK a deep breath and made my way back to the pawn-shop. On the backside of the building, a set of rickety metal steps led to a landing flanked with two black doors. There were two balconies, one overflowing with colorful flowers and the other empty.

I stared up at the landing for a few minutes, jumping when a sharp voice startled me. "You lost?"

A petite woman in a long, flowing skirt stepped out of an apartment doorway, her strawberry blonde hair tousled. Streaks of green and purple paint covered her arms, adding to the hippie vibe.

"I'm not sure." I stepped away from the sidewalk and hastened toward her. "Ian said I could stay here for a few days. I'm not sure which apartment he meant."

The woman nodded and pointed toward the other door. "Two's the only one that's available. Guess he meant for you to go there."

My gaze swept the area around the pawnshop. "I thought he had a room for me to rent. I'm not sure—"

She laughed, a rusty sound that made me flinch. "It's clean. Everything works. Got a bathroom and everything, although you'll need to do your laundry down the street."

I noted the chipping paint on the closed door and the rusted number two hanging at an angle from a nail. "I don't know if I'm supposed to be here."

"If he offered you the place, there must be a reason. That's Ian. Patron Saint of Loose Women and Lost Causes." She inclined her head and studied me for a moment. "Which are you?"

I smoothed my hand down the front of my sundress. While wrinkled and unkempt from being balled up in my suitcase, it was not revealing in the least. "I don't think I'm either."

"Lost cause, then. Tramps will usually self-identify." She turned to go back into her apartment, her skirt swirling behind her. "I'm Josie. Let me know if you need anything. I'm always here." She laughed as if telling herself a joke and then closed the door. The lock engaged with a sharp *click*.

I swept a gaze around the landing. Although the back side of the building had a relaxing view of the water, it wasn't in the best area of town. Nearby buildings had bars over their doors. A dumpster overflowing with black garbage bags hulked directly outside the apartment. A boat was tied to the dock nearby, but even it looked like it had seen sunnier days.

It was this or Beverlee's love nest, though, so I let myself in the door.

I expected a trash-filled dump, but the apartment was fresh and clean. Instead of dirty brown linoleum, the cheery decor reminded me of a vintage ice cream shop. Light aqua paint covered the walls, and the glossy white cabinets sparkled. Even the dining table resembled something off a postcard from the 1950s. Bright red vinyl benches trimmed in shiny metal flanked the table, and yellow curtains spotted with red poppies blew gently with the breeze from the open door.

I was about to fetch my things from the car when a noise came from the open doorway. I jerked around, expecting a crash course in neighborhood danger. Instead, a fluffy golden retriever sat near the door holding a gnarled, wet tennis ball in his mouth.

I had always loved dogs, but Cobb would never allow one in the house. Too needy, he said, like needing somebody was a character flaw. This guy seemed friendly, though, so in a moment of defiance of my ex, I took a few tentative steps toward the door.

"Are you my neighbor?" I asked as he leaned in for a sniff.

He tilted his head like he was trying to understand me. When I gave him a scratch behind the ear, his foot thumped against the floor. The sound echoed across the landing.

Josie's door opened, and she stuck her head out. When he saw her, the dog jumped up and bounded to her side.

"I see you've met Rusty," she said. "He's our neighborhood mascot."

"Is he yours?" I asked.

She chuckled, then leaned down and kissed the top of the dog's head. "He belongs to Ian as much as anybody. But if you share your take-out and throw the ball with him, he'll be your best friend."

My heart banged against the wall of my chest. "Ian lives here?"

"He didn't tell you?" She pointed to the sailboat tied up a mere thirty feet from her door. "He lives on that boat. He's practically your roommate."

5
_____

I had just finished unpacking my suitcase into a small wooden dresser and was considering heating a can of tomato soup I found abandoned in the kitchen cabinet when Beverlee called. "I had the most wonderful lunch," she said with a sigh. "Are you still out running your errands? We have a lot to do this afternoon."

"Funny you should ask. I ran into Scoots. We talked about your big news and she offered me a place to stay until the wedding."

I wasn't comfortable throwing Scoots under the bus, but I was even less comfortable with the guilt trip Beverlee would throw my way if she thought finding another place to stay was my idea. And besides, Scoots was a big girl and probably had access to a variety of weapons. She'd be able to handle Beverlee far better than I could.

"I'll be nearby to help," I continued. "But you and Edwin need to enjoy your wedding preparations without being interrupted. This is your special time."

"You're right," she said. "This is my special time and I

should have what I want. And what I want is you back here where you belong."

I imagined Beverlee petulantly stomping her size six heels and rubbed the back of my hand over my closed eyelids, trying to figure out a way past her special brand of hand-me-down Southern reproach.

"Glory, baby, you are family," she said, her tone quickly shifting from a grumble to a whine. "What do you have to lose by coming home?"

My dignity, for one. My self-respect. And also my ability to sleep at night without something stuck in my ear canals to keep me from hearing things I'd never erase from my memory.

But two could play at this game of emotional manipulation, so I exhaled and kept my voice even. "I need... space, Beverlee. To finish my wallow in peace. You understand, right?"

If anyone knew the value of post-breakup solitude, it was Beverlee. I held my breath and crossed my fingers, waiting for her response.

After several seconds, she channeled her inner Southern guilt fairy and sighed dramatically. "Fine. At least you're here."

"Exactly. I'm so close. Right down the road." Eager to change the subject before she tried to talk me out of it, I added, "What's on our list for today?"

Suitably distracted, she rattled off a list of things she wanted to accomplish, finally ending in, "And then we'll run by the wedding planner's office. I need to get a copy of everything she had so we can move forward without her."

"I've been thinking about that. Can you bring me a copy of your contract with Doris?"

I knew from experience that whatever happened with the

details of Beverlee's ceremony would be determined by what was in that document.

"My contract?" Beverlee asked, her voice rising in confusion.

"Yes, what did your contract with Doris say?"

"I'm not sure, to be honest. Our first meeting with her ran long, and I had a manicure appointment to get to. I left Edwin to handle the financial details."

I rubbed the back of my neck. "Beverlee, it's possible you still owe Doris or her company money for the wedding."

Beverlee gasped. "I refuse to pay a dead woman, Glory."

"Then we need to get our hands on the contract so we can see what we're up against."

She murmured her agreement. "I have a folder full of pictures from Pinterest, a couple of rough menus, and some quick notes from our meetings, but I don't have any official paperwork. Let's go see her assistant. I'm sure she has a copy."

"Beverlee," I said, paging through Doris's wedding website on my phone from the passenger seat of the car after she picked me up. "You didn't tell me we were talking about Maggie."

Magnolia Winters had been a pain in my behind since she tripped me on the playground when I was five, and then, as I lay wiping pea gravel out of my mouth and from my skinned knee, pointed out I was wearing purple butterfly underwear to the entire kindergarten class. Her humiliation tactics had matured over the years, but my desire for her to get what was coming to her hadn't.

"Well, yes. Maggie has worked for Doris for the last several years," she said, nodding. "I never liked that girl. Do you remember how she acted when she tricked Ian into taking her to the homecoming dance your senior year?"

"No," I said, the heat rising in my cheeks like it always did when I thought back to Ian and Maggie together, but wanting to avoid this trip down memory lane. "I don't remember."

"Sure you do, honey. She had a picture of the two of them blown up and put on the wall of her mama's café. You couldn't eat a chicken wing in this town without seeing them smiling down on you. You don't remember?"

I gritted my teeth, a buzzing sensation building in the back of my skull. "Nope. Not ringing any bells."

"Well, I do," Beverlee said, pointing a bright red lacquered fingernail toward my face. "You used to get so upset about it you refused to even eat there anymore. And since it was the only restaurant in town back then, we went a good six months without getting decent food. Made me cook at home." She patted her stomach. "Which, come to think of it, might have been the start of my career."

Beverlee leaned in with a whisper as she pulled the convertible to a stop. "Are you up for this, baby? I know there's a lot of history here."

I bit my bottom lip. After everything Beverlee had done for me, the least I could do was play nice with Maggie Winters, even if she was one of the people I hated most in the world.

WEDDINGS by the Sea was located in a white building on the edge of the town's main beach access road. It was perfectly situated to attract both tourists who wanted a destination wedding and locals who wanted an upscale ceremony. The ocean was minutes away, and this area of Flat Falls had the picturesque small-town charm you'd find on the pages of a brochure for romantic getaways.

A thin layer of sand dusted the walkway in front of the building, and the window box out front contained flowers in varying shades of pink and white. Windsocks shaped like pastel seahorses danced from the rafters above the door. It was cute and classy, like a wedding planning business should be, and I fought the urge to pluck one of Maggie's begonias from its stem out of spite.

Beverlee pushed open the front door, a bell inside signaling our arrival. "Hello," she called. "Anybody here?" When nobody answered, she motioned for me to take a seat in the waiting room. "We'll wait."

I followed her and halted inside an inviting entryway decorated like the inside of a fashion magazine. White leather couches formed a seating arrangement off to one side, each flanked by a glass and chrome table with two flawless arrangements of light purple irises. A coffee table held two symmetrical stacks of high-end wedding magazines, which I nudged off-center with my knee when I walked by.

I sat down next to Beverlee on one of the sofas, and it made the kind of low groaning sound that would have people around you thinking you'd passed gas. I looked over at Beverlee in alarm, relieved she didn't seem to notice.

"Fancy place, isn't it?" she whispered and flipped through a glossy brochure she had picked up from the side table.

"A little uptight, if you ask me." I crossed my arms in front of my chest. I knew I was being petulant, but Maggie had been the source of more than a few of my tears growing up, and the twelve-year-old still sulking inside me wasn't ready to let the resentment go.

With a loud click, an interior door opened, and Maggie entered the room. A toilet flushed behind her and, for a moment, I imagined a world where we each had a sound effect that played every time we made an entrance. Since she once flashed around a Polaroid of me crying in the middle school bathroom after nobody invited me to the Fall Fling, I figured a toilet was appropriate for Maggie.

She strolled toward us, extending her hand. "I'm so sorry, I—" When she recognized us, her hand fell to her side, and her eyes narrowed. "Hello, Beverlee," she said and nodded toward me with a chilly glare. "Glory."

I stood and grinned, pushing down the sting of embarrassing memories that always popped up around her. "Well, hey there, Magnolia." She hated being called by her given name, so I used it every chance I got. "Nice place you've got here."

Maggie stared at me, her mouth formed into a perfect oval and a delightful look of confusion spread across her face. Then she straightened the magazines on the table.

Beverlee cleared her throat and smacked the brochure on the sofa, snapping Maggie back to reality. She turned her head. "Beverlee, I understand you've got quite the unusual wedding planned. Brides of a certain age tend to get... creative." She raised a manicured brow and plastered on a fake smile that showed an excessive number of her too-straight teeth. "But I haven't ever heard of someone wanting to get married on a pirate ship. Interesting choice."

My pulse quickened, and I leaned forward, finally ready to put Maggie in her place, but Beverlee's arm snaked across my leg, its weight rooting me to the seat with firm pressure. "Well, some of us are lucky enough to find men with a sense of adventure." Beverlee smiled, sweet Southern sarcasm dripping from her words. "While some of us stay single until we shrivel up like prunes."

Beverlee lowered her voice to a whisper. "And we all know prunes are only useful when you need some dedicated time in the ladies' room."

She gave a pointed stare toward the bathroom and I tried not to flinch at Beverlee's obvious disdain for the single ladies in the room. Sometimes she went overboard with her love for all things wedding and failed to notice that not everybody was so in love with love.

Maggie squared her shoulders, a muscle twitching in her jaw. "Did you come here for a reason or just to insult me?"

Insulting her was a bonus. I coughed into my hand to hide my smirk. "We're so very sorry for your loss," I said. "Terrible. Just terrible."

Maggie tilted her head and narrowed her glare, her gaze focused on me with clear disdain. "I heard you were the one who found the body."

I flashed again to the picture of Doris from last night. The one that wouldn't leave the darkest part of my mind. I swallowed against the acrid sting of bile rising in my throat.

Beverlee gave my leg a squeeze and stood. "Yes, it was quite a shock. But I'm afraid Doris's death has left us in a bit of a bind."

"Oh?" Maggie pursed her lips and her brows lifted another half an inch.

I dipped my chin. "As you know, Beverlee's wedding is coming up soon. I'd like to see Doris's files since we will be scrambling to get everything done in time."

Maggie crossed to one of the glossy white tables on the other side of the room and bent over a filing cabinet. She pushed aside a full package of gourmet Belgian chocolates, a bag of saltwater taffy, and a half-eaten peanut butter cup before she started rifling through the files. She pulled one out, placing it flat on the desk in front of Beverlee. When she flipped it open with the end of her fingernail, the folder was empty. "As you can see, there's nothing here."

"Can we at least see a copy of the contract?" I asked.

Maggie leaned over the desk and logged into the

computer. After clicking through the directory, she straightened up and said, "I'm sorry, but it doesn't look like there's an electronic copy, either."

I glanced at Beverlee and lifted a shoulder. "No contract, no problem."

I looked slowly around the room, not buying for a minute that there weren't any files. "Something just occurred to me, Magnolia. Now that Doris is gone, who owns the business?"

Maggie took a step back, her brows wrinkling. She smoothed out the front of her skirt. "I suppose I do, if I want it. Doris was grooming me to take over for her. I have the option to purchase it in the event she is no longer a… viable owner."

"Isn't that interesting, Beverlee? What a way to get control of a business. Imagine, one day you're a lowly employee and then, poof…" I waved my hand in the air like a magician. "You're the owner."

"What are you trying to suggest?" Maggie asked, her face growing pale.

Beverlee patted Maggie's hand. "She's just thinking how uncomfortable that conversation will be, once the police put pieces together."

As if on cue, the door chimed, and Hollis Goodnight strode into the shop. "Hello, ladies. Are you doing a little wedding planning today?"

I tossed a wink toward Maggie and closed the folder on the table. "No, Chief Goodnight, we were about to leave. I'll bet you and Maggie have a few interesting things to chat about."

Maggie's eyes widened, and Beverlee waved back over her shoulder. "Don't you worry about our wedding plans, honey. You've got a lot on your plate now with running this ritzy business by yourself. We've got the wedding under control."

If anyone around this town was capable of murder, I'd put money on the former Miss Flat Falls, with her silky blond hair and baby blues. I pictured her mile-long legs being tucked into a police car and found myself more cheerful than I had been all day.

6

Beverlee seized my arm, half-dragging me to the car. "How do you feel about taking over as my wedding planner? Sure, you haven't done many events since Cobb left, but it's not like you don't know what to do."

I recalled the humiliation of the last event I organized. What started as a black-tie charity auction filled with the elite members of Raleigh's social scene had ended in disaster. Instead of handing off a heavy box of cash at the end of the night, I sat in a holding cell explaining to my client and the police that my husband was both a con man and a thief. "If you remember correctly, my last event was a complete failure," I said.

Beverlee nodded and opened the car door, pushing me into the passenger seat. "Watch your head." She rounded the convertible and settled onto the seat next to me. "So, you had a bad party."

"A bad party? My husband ran off with a seventeen-thousand-dollar cash box during the most important event of my career." My voice was getting shrill. "I was forced to empty my bank account and sell my dining room furniture to pay the client back. It was on the news, and I was lucky they didn't press charges. That's more than just a bad party, Bev."

She patted my knee as she eased the car out of its parking space. "You know what they say: if you fall off a horse, the best cure is to get back up and ride again. And besides, that ugly table didn't suit you at all. Frankly, I'm glad you're rid of it."

I squeezed my hands together. Beverlee would keel over if she figured out the only furniture left in my house was a twenty-dollar sofa from the thrift store to replace the one I'd sold to pay the water bill. It smelled like cheap Chinese food leftovers and looked like thirty-year-old kitchen wallpaper. "Being the laughingstock of the whole town is a little more than falling off a horse."

She grunted. "Only if you let it be."

I stared out the window for a few minutes until I realized we weren't heading back to Beverlee's house. She drove past old fishing shacks and the marina, then turned down a tree-lined street that ran parallel to the water. "Where are we going?"

"Well, Edwin texted me when we were in with Maggie and said there was still police tape on the boat when he jogged by there this morning."

She pulled the car to a stop in front of a pier lined with upscale yachts. Compared to Old Bill's boat, these boats made me smile. They were well-kept and expensive, and it would be much easier to plan a wedding ceremony on one of their expansive decks. "You found another ship to have your ceremony on?" I asked, letting the first sliver of hope I'd had in days slide over me.

She sighed. "Oh, don't be silly. These boats don't have the same character."

"Then why are we here?" My jaw ached from clenching my teeth.

She answered by turning the engine off and jumping out. "Come on. There is someone I need to talk to."

I trailed along behind Beverlee. As we approached the last boat on the dock, I could hear the thump of music and a loud whirring sound. "Oh good," Beverlee said. "We're not too late for supper."

Unlike the decrepit boat where Doris met her maker, this yacht featured glossy teak and shiny fiberglass, with a freshly painted hull and bright brass fixtures. Whoever lived there was swimming in money and probably had a full-time crew that wore crisp white linen and always carried a tray of champagne flutes topped with raspberries.

The hatch flung open and Scoots poked her head out, a red bandana wrapped around her neck and shiny silver hoops dangling from her ears. She raised a margarita glass toward us. "Well, this is a welcome surprise." She waved us onboard and stuck the glass in my hand.

I eyed the drink in surprise. "Is this what I think it is?"

Scoots grinned. "Margaritas. Dinner of champions."

I expected Beverlee to explain why we were here. Instead, she pushed the glass toward my lips.

I shook my head and held the drink out to her. I needed to keep a clear mind to process everything that had been happening. "You drink it."

"None for me, I'm driving," she said, not bothering to hide her chuckle. "But if you're worried about it, consider it a grown-up lime smoothie."

"If I thought I would have visitors, I'd have made a bigger batch." Scoots nodded to the captain's chair on the deck. "Have a seat, drink up, and spill the details. I want to hear all about Doris the piñata."

SCOOTS LEANED FORWARD and listened to Beverlee replay the events from the night before. She stuck her pointer finger out from its position on the glass and motioned toward us. "Maybe this is a sign that you should elope. Or not get married at all. Nobody would blink an eye these days if they found out you and Edwin were living in sin."

Beverlee clapped twice. "Nonsense. I love a good wedding. But since that old biddy got herself axed, I need help with a few minor details. Glory here's an expert at events, but she's not familiar with Flat Falls anymore and she doesn't have your connections. I know you like a good party as much as I do, so we stopped by to see if you have any suggestions."

"You keep talking about how inconvenient Doris's death was." Scoots narrowed her eyes at Beverlee. "Did you have anything to do with it?"

Beverlee coughed. "Can't say I didn't want to throw her overboard a time or two. But, no. This one wasn't me."

"What do you mean 'this one'?" I asked, pressing my fingers together until the skin blanched. "Hollis already thinks you had something to do with Doris and that boat. Please tell me you're kidding."

Beverlee pried my hands apart and shoved the now empty glass back into it. "Don't you worry about that, honey."

Scoots disappeared down below and returned with a legal pad and pen. She grinned at Beverlee. "Looks like we have a wedding to plan. Item number one, find a location without a dead body."

Beverlee nodded her agreement. "But don't limit our options right off the bat. I'm not opposed to a little character."

Scoots scribbled on the pad. "Duly noted. Item one A:

Client prefers a crime scene-free location but is open to other options."

Beverlee leaned over toward me with a conspiratorial whisper. "She used to be a lawyer. Lists get her all hot and bothered."

"Hold on. I'm confused." I pointed at Scoots. "You're a lawyer?"

"Haven't practiced in decades, but yes." She nodded toward the open water. "Turns out there's more to life than working in a stuffy courtroom."

I pondered how to ask the obvious question without seeming rude. "So, you're a former lawyer with a side gig running a pawnshop."

"Do you remember my husband?" Scoots asked.

I thought back to my childhood. "George? The guy with the bushy orange beard who owned all that real estate downtown? He disappeared. Did he…?"

"No, he didn't die, but I'm sure he wished it for a while. Turns out he couldn't keep it in his pants." She cast her wistful gaze over the water. "Next to his mistresses, he loved this boat more than anything in the world." She grinned. "Lesson number one, child: don't divorce a lawyer with a chip on her shoulder. You'll lose every time."

"So, you live on this boat like a pirate?"

"I live on this boat like a woman who won't be taken advantage of again." She pulled out her phone and took a few pictures of me. "But I make sure to send George snapshots of everything he's missing."

"Like afternoon margaritas?" I suggested.

"Afternoon margaritas being sipped on by a hottie half his age. His specialty." She snickered. "He'll need an extra heart pill tonight, for sure."

I gestured around the boat. "So, this is your revenge ship?"

One side of her mouth tilted up, and she wiggled her brows. "It started out that way. But then I decided I like who I am when I'm on the water."

"A pirate?"

Scoots speared me with an annoyed glare. "Do I have greasy hair? Bad teeth? Do I look uncivilized to you?"

I shook my head.

She lifted her empty margarita glass. "Present beverage notwithstanding, of course."

I wasn't sure how to respond, so I nodded in agreement.

"Being a pirate wouldn't be all bad, though. Pirates take what they want. They're not afraid to be bold." She shook her pointer finger at me. "You only get one life, kiddo, and it's a lot more fun when you stop worrying so much about other people's opinions."

"And that, my dear, is why Edwin and I will have a pirate wedding," Beverlee said, dabbing a tissue at the corner of her eye. "Because love is wild. And I'm wild, too. And it turns out that's okay."

I couldn't argue with that.

After our liquid afternoon snack, Beverlee motioned for us to follow her to her car. I climbed into the back seat of the convertible behind them. "Where are we going now?"

"If your aunt has her heart set on that boat, then we're going to make it happen for her."

"It's a crime scene, Scoots."

She scoffed. "Life is a crime scene, sweetie. Minor inconvenience."

My fingers gripped the armrest as trailers and beach shops flew past the window. I couldn't see the speedometer, but I was fairly certain Beverlee broke sixty before we even left the parking lot.

I was just about to ask Beverlee to slow down when she came to a screeching halt in front of the dock leading to Old

Bill's boat. There were already two police cars and a dark sedan parked nearby. "Um, guys? I don't think this is the best time to—"

"Nonsense, it's always a good time to witness our criminal justice system at work," Scoots declared as she hopped out of the car. She was surprisingly nimble for somebody pushing seventy.

I trailed Beverlee and Scoots as they approached the boat. It wasn't as scary during the day, but it would take a lot more than sunshine to make me forget what had happened here. I stepped over a knobby piece of driftwood next to the walkway and turned when a man's voice boomed from the other side of the boat.

"I don't care who you are. You need to get the hell off my boat so I can do my job." Old Bill Judson lumbered into view, followed closely by Hollis.

"Bill, I understand you're frustrated," Hollis used his don't-make-me-shoot-you voice. I knew it well. He pointed out over the water, now choppy with an incoming storm. "You won't catch anything this morning, anyway. Might as well let us do our jobs. The sooner we're finished, the sooner you can get back to your normal life."

The first time I met Old Bill, I was in sixth grade and had to write a report on *The Old Man and the Sea*. I tried asking him questions about what it was like to be a ship's captain, but he grunted and ordered me to get off his property. He hadn't changed much since then. His ruddy cheeks still crinkled like paper grocery sacks, his flyaway eyebrow hairs stretching in different directions like they always had.

He jabbed a gnarled finger toward me. "What's that one doing here? She a part of this?"

I raised a hand in return. "Hey, Mr. Judson, it's me, Glory Wells."

"I know who you are, girl. I'm asking why you're here."

Just then, Beverlee motioned for the police chief to come closer. "Hollis, if I might have a word." She squinted toward Bill, who was still watching us with an agitated glare. "I have a theory."

She thought Old Bill Judson, who was no spring chicken at close to eighty-five years old, had strung Doris up from the side of his own boat. "Beverlee, seriously? He's about eight minutes from kicking the bucket himself."

"Hear me out," she whispered. "I came by one day last week to talk to him about using the boat for the wedding. He acted shifty and tried to get me out of here. I know he could use the money, but he didn't even want to talk about it. He's hiding something."

"Or maybe he doesn't like you," Hollis suggested.

Beverlee sent him a confused look. "What on earth do you mean? Why wouldn't he like me?"

"Or maybe he wanted to be left alone," I said.

"I didn't invite him to brunch, Glory. I simply wanted to use his boat for a party. But he wouldn't even talk to me about it. Kept shooing me away and glancing over his shoulder like he was nervous about something. All I'm saying is that we should check him out. I think there's more to this story than we know."

I swung around to see Old Bill standing near the side of his boat, eyes narrowed and focused on us.

A shiver crawled up my spine, and I wondered if Beverlee was right. What if Old Bill Judson was the murderer?

7

"I hate to say it," Scoots muttered as we drove away from Old Bill's boat. "But I think we'll have to find another location for your wedding."

Beverlee veered the car over to the side of the road and put it in park. She faced Scoots and sat there, unblinking, wordlessly offering what she used to refer to as a "clarifying moment."

I shifted in my seat uncomfortably. I had fallen into Beverlee's trap more times than I could count over the years, and Scoots had two choices: she'd either see the error of her ways, or she would walk home.

After several long moments, Scoots finally raised a brow and cocked her head to the side. "Does that usually work for you? Because I've been doing these Kegel exercises I found on the Internet, and I'm fairly sure my bladder and I can sit here all day."

I gaped at the woman in the front seat and debated giving her a high five. If I had known defying Beverlee was an option, my adolescent years would have looked a lot different.

Beverlee grunted, peered over her shoulder, and pulled the car back onto the road. She drove without speaking for several miles, which was akin to a month-long vow of silence for most other people. I was just starting to wonder if the apocalypse was coming when she squinted at me in the rearview mirror and said, "Where to?"

I dipped my chin. "I could eat."

With a nod, she turned right at the next corner. "Fat Hectors it is, then."

Fat Hectors was a Mexican cantina occupying the darkest recesses of a strip mall in the town's center for decades. I was relieved to discover updated décor including bright murals and swaths of fabric in dark reds and oranges. Punched tin stars, suspended from the ceiling by thin strands of translucent fishing line, cast tiny spots of light throughout the room.

Fat Hector himself greeted us when we walked in. He was a string bean of a man, almost seven feet tall, and although his hair had begun to gray at the temples, he still looked the same as he had a decade earlier when Ian and I ate there before our senior prom.

"I was beginning to think the rumor mill let me down," he said with a hearty chuckle, scooping me up in a hug. "Because certainly my Glory wouldn't come back into town and wait for days before paying me a visit."

I scuffed the floor with my toe before grinning up at him. "It's good to see you, Hector."

He leaned forward in a half-bow. "Will you be joining us at The Beach this evening?"

Fat Hectors sat in arguably one of the worst locations in town, but he refused to pay for a more desirable waterfront restaurant space. Instead, he paid a high school kid a hundred bucks to drive his pickup truck to the beach a dozen times to deliver loads of "authentic ocean sand" to the parking lot behind the building and he piled it in the corner beside plastic kiddie pools and a row of tiki torches. Half a dozen tables rested on a flat area of artificial turf, and the bar was perched on wheels so Hector could roll it into a supply closet if the health inspector stopped by unannounced.

Strictly off-limits to tourists, The Beach had no menu. If you dined there, you trusted Hector to cook whatever he wanted you to eat. And Fat Hector had never done me wrong.

We followed him down the long corridor, and he opened the emergency exit with a flourish. "It's good to have you back," he whispered in my ear before he pointed toward an open table near the edge of the sand. "Things were awfully boring around here without you."

I had a hard time believing that. As soon as she stepped out onto the patio, Beverlee was surrounded by several neighbors wanting to talk to her about what it was like to find a dead body.

Beverlee had always been a semi-celebrity in Flat Falls, usually causing a stir wherever she went. It wasn't uncommon for half a restaurant to abandon their tables to greet her when she came in to eat.

But when a table of women on the far side of the patio turned their backs to her, closing off their circle of chairs with whispered mumbles, I realized not everybody in town was rallying behind her.

I approached Beverlee from behind, trying to slide into the chair next to Scoots without my aunt turning her head and noticing the snub from across the courtyard.

As soon as she spotted me, though, Beverlee grinned and jabbed a finger toward the woman standing next to her. "Glory, you remember Nurse Nikki, right? From the podiatrist's office? She was just telling me that her husband, who works nights at the gas station, found out from his second cousin that Doris Sadler was an FBI agent, and that she was killed in a drug cartel hit right here in Flat Falls. It explains why she was so standoffish. It must be hard to make friends when you're undercover."

Nurse Nikki was dressed in a tight tennis dress and knee-high argyle socks and had her long hair pulled up in pigtails, so she clearly wasn't a reliable source. And the way her gaze shifted around the room when she talked, like she was expecting a hidden camera to burst out from behind the life-sized plastic cactus, made me wonder what she was hiding.

I slid my gaze around the patio. Everybody out there was hiding something. I could see it in their hunched shoulders and the way they tossed not-so-subtle frowns at each other like moldy fish sticks.

Any one of those people could have killed Doris Sadler.

"I heard she went into the Piggly Wiggly last week and bought nothing but champagne, a box of paper clips, and three canisters of whipped cream," another woman said, waving a tortilla chip in the air as she spoke. "Who knows what kind of ritual sacrifice she was about to perform with those."

I pinched the bridge of my nose and willed the talking to stop. Doris was about as close to being an FBI agent as I was, and I had received far stranger requests than to pick up a stash of alcohol and office supplies for my clients during my event planning days.

We were saved from hearing the pharmacist's alien invasion theories when Hector brought out a tray of chorizo and potato flautas topped with crema and a pitcher of pink lemonade sangria adorned with fresh peach and candied lemon slices.

"No more talking," Scoots said over a mouthful of food, a hard scowl aimed at the other patrons. "Let us eat in peace."

The crowd slowly dissipated, but I felt uneasy at both the rumors already making their way through town and my sudden propensity to view everybody I came across as a potential murderer.

∼

I RETURNED HOME that evening to find Josie on the front stoop of the building, legs crossed, and a sketchbook balanced in her lap. I smiled as I stepped around her but stopped when she posed a soft question. "Did you find what you were looking for?"

I turned and straightened my spine. "What makes you think I'm looking for something?"

The stack of metal bracelets on her arm jingled as she shrugged. "Just a hunch. You showed up and things around here got interesting."

"And you concluded that I'm on the hunt for some-thing?" Small-town logic was one reason I'd left town the first time.

She stared at me for a few seconds, then laughed. "No, but my dry cleaner's son delivered my laundry today, and you and your aunt have gotten the gossip nest around here all stirred up. Last I heard, the two of you were interrogating suspects at knifepoint."

I frowned, irked that the town chatter now included me and my fledgling investigation. "Do you always believe things your delivery drivers tell you?"

"Mostly. Except for the pizza guy. I don't trust him."

My skin prickled with irritation. "If you like gossip so much, why don't you go get it yourself instead of relying on people to bring it to your doorstep?"

Josie lifted the hem of her dress to display a small black box attached to her ankle by a thick nylon strap. "Maybe I will, in about one hundred and twenty-five days and a few odd hours."

I stepped back. I had never met someone with an ankle monitor and wondered what kind of crime she committed to get one. Murder? Robbery? "You're under house arrest and you gossiped about me?"

Josie seemed nice enough, but I had watched enough stories on the news over the years to know that sometimes the bad guys didn't wear black and look like gunslingers. Sometimes they were the nice ones, the neighbors everybody described as quiet and polite. I gave a placating smile and positioned myself to run if necessary.

Josie's rusty laugh scraped my ears. "It's much more fun to talk about other people's drama than to take a deep dive into my own."

It didn't appear Josie was an imminent threat, so the nosy gene won out again. "Did you... I mean, what..."

"Didn't kill anybody, if that's what you were wondering."

"I wasn't," I said quickly, hoping she couldn't see through my lie. "You wouldn't be sitting here at the beach if you were a murderer." I backed up another half-step. "At least I don't think so."

Josie tilted her head and arched a brow. "Have you ever had someone turn out to be not who they seemed?"

I chuckled. "Yes. Yes, I have."

Josie patted the front stoop, inviting me to sit. "Want to talk about it? Sometimes it helps to tell a friend. And I'm not going anywhere for a while."

I glanced over my shoulder at my car, debating whether to make a run for it. But I didn't have many friends left, and she seemed nice enough, even if she was a criminal with a penchant for gossip. I dropped my bag on the steps and sat down next to her.

Thirty minutes later, after Josie had disappeared into her

apartment and returned with a box of wine and a plate of cookies, I had spilled the entire story.

"What you're saying is that your perfect husband lied?" Josie smirked at me. "Shocker." She sighed and pushed the plate of cookies toward me. "What are you going to do?"

"Well, I'll get my aunt married off, for one. But it looks like I can't do that until I figure out who killed the wedding planner. It seems like everybody in Flat Falls is a closet criminal."

I cringed at my tactless remark, but Josie just bit into her cookie Over a mouthful of crumbs, she said, "The kid who delivered my groceries this morning said he was dropping some sandwiches off at the police station and overheard them say your aunt was the main suspect. I can't imagine it would be fun to plan a wedding with the cops breathing down your neck."

My stomach fell. She was talking about Beverlee, the woman who had accepted me into her home as a lost and scared orphan with nowhere else to go. The woman who had put her entire Technicolor life on hold to raise me and love me even when I was a belligerent and rebellious teenager, and the one who just welcomed me back home like my big city vanishing act hadn't broken her heart.

Beverlee was a lot of things, but she wasn't a murderer.

And I owed it to her to find the proof to show the world she was innocent.

8

On Wednesday morning, I pushed open the door to the only breakfast restaurant in Flat Falls. Settled in the warehouse district near the waterfront docks, its wide plank maple floors scuffed from years of sandy flip-flops and straw bags overflowing with sunscreen and beach pails, the Grind and Go remained part café and part central hub for town gossip.

I breathed in the scent of coffee and cinnamon rolls and glanced around the room. With its exposed brick walls and mismatched ladder-back chairs, the Grind and Go could have been trendy. But instead of softly lit photos of hipster latte art, an enormous mural of vintage David Hasselhoff, complete with winged eighties hair and surrounded by fluorescent hearts and shooting stars, lined the back wall.

I had been hoping for a few quiet moments to gather my thoughts before starting on Beverlee's marathon wedding planning itinerary, but I should have known better. Every table in the café was taken.

I had just turned to leave when the woman behind the counter shouted out a greeting.

Shirley Ladetto had been flipping pancakes and burning sausage here for as long as I could remember. Like the mural behind her, which stood as a testament to the power of a post-divorce one- night stand she swore she had when the actor was on the coast filming a movie, Shirley still lived a few decades behind the rest of us.

But even in her frosted denim overalls, a yellow scrunchie holding back auburn hair streaked with gray, she commanded attention. "Hey everybody," she hollered, slapping the butcher block counter with her palm. "Look who's back in town."

Several people muttered hellos, and I gave a half-hearted wave in return. "Good morning."

I recognized a few faces. My high school principal was sitting in the corner, probably awaiting an apology for hurling a pencil sharpener through his office window after he gave me detention. Again.

A woman who looked like my old mail carrier was ordering at the counter and gave me the side-eye. And she wasn't the only one. Everybody in the place was either staring or avoiding eye contact, but even though I had lived in Flat Falls for the first eighteen years of my life, not a single person invited me to sit with them. Not one for subtlety, Shirley let out a shrill whistle. "Somebody make room. Now."

Still nobody moved. One woman I didn't recognize loudly asked, "Isn't that the murder lady?"

My cheeks flamed, and I backed toward the door. I didn't like being reminded of the crime, and I didn't want everybody to think of a dead body every time they saw me. "I'm going to—"

Before I could finish, a warm hand clamped around my wrist. Ian. Wonderful. Nothing enhanced humiliation more than having it happen in front of your ex.

Instead of smirking, though, he motioned for me to sit

down. He took a slow sip of his coffee. "I was supposed to be having breakfast with my sister, but she couldn't make it. The seat's yours if you want it."

I didn't trust myself to speak, so I simply nodded.

Shirley ambled up and plunked a cup of coffee on the table. It had already been laced with generous amounts of cream and sugar. "If I remember correctly, and I usually do, you like cinnamon pancakes with extra pecans and a side of bacon, extra crispy. Anything else?"

My stomach rumbled in response, and I was touched she remembered my favorite breakfast after all these years. Maybe all the memories people around here had weren't bad. "Sounds wonderful."

After she walked away, I turned to Ian. "Not much has changed here."

He ran the pad of his thumb across my empty ring finger. "You're not wearing a wedding band. That's a change."

Warmth climbed my cheeks. "No wedding band. No husband. But you already knew that."

"The Flat Falls rumor mill is alive and well, as I'm sure you've already seen. Three separate people have taken it upon themselves to come into the bar and ask me about the 'pretty lady' staying in my apartment. I don't have the heart to tell them who you really are."

I leaned back in my chair, irritation taking up residence next to the embarrassment already prickling on my cheeks. "And who am I, Ian?"

He didn't respond. Instead, he took a long sip of coffee and stared out the window.

I was about to give up when he said gruffly, "I'm sorry things didn't work out the way you wanted."

"Come on. Let's not pretend you're sad about my heartbreak. I got what was coming to me, right?"

"Is that what you think? That I'd gloat when someone I cared about got hurt?"

I tilted my head and chuckled. "I'm sure you lost a lot of sleep over it."

A dimple flashed in his cheek. It was only there for a second, but I found myself mesmerized by it and the memories that came along with it.

"Okay, there might have been a moment of satisfaction. I'm only human." His voice got quiet. "I'm sorry. Really. I want to find the jerk that broke your heart and put my fist through his face."

"Yeah, you'd need to get in line behind my aunt. And me."

I tore off a corner of the paper napkin in my lap, my eyes focused on David Hasselhoff's smirk from the back wall. My marriage to Cobb Mulvaney ended in much the same way it began, with the sharp sting of humiliation and a heart suddenly robbed of everything it thought was true.

The morning I met Cobb, I had only been in Raleigh for six months, and I still hadn't gotten used to the rhythm of city life. Every morning, I lugged my backpack to the library for an Internet search of job listings and e-mail responses, hoping one of the town's event planners had miraculously decided to give a girl from the middle of nowhere a shot at her dream life.

I had just stepped into the alley next to the library, rain plastering my hair to my face and defeat on my mind, when a beat-up Jeep screeched down the narrow road and came to a thudding halt inches away from my thigh.

I jerked my head up and lost my footing, landing with a splash in a muddy pothole, my pants caked in grime and my ego bruised.

Cobb had jumped out of the car like a gallant knight in a dirty chef's coat and picked me up from the ground, wiped off my tears, and coaxed me into a nearby coffee shop for a cup of Earl Grey and a brownie. He listened to my stories and, for the first time since I had left Flat Falls, made me feel like everything might turn out all right.

We got married six months later.

And for a while, things were good. When we were together, he said all the right things, made all the gestures. When he'd come home from a shift at the restaurant, he always had flowers in hand and pretty words to explain why he was later than normal or all of a sudden smelled like cheap drugstore perfume instead of smoky barbecue and stale beer.

Or when our checking account was missing a zero or two, and he'd sweep me away for a weekend in the mountains instead of answering my questions.

I thought he was the best thing that had ever happened to me.

Spoiler alert: he wasn't.

"You haven't seen him since he left?" Ian asked, dragging my attention back to the worn wood table. His fingers were curled around the edge.

"No, he pretty much vanished." With my savings, my dignity, and a good-sized chunk of my heart. "The police tried looking for him for a few months, but never got any leads. He was here one day and then…" I waved my hand in the air. "Poof. Gone, just like that."

"Have you tried finding him yourself? You could hire a private investigator."

I didn't have enough money to add guacamole to my tacos, much less hire a private investigator. "Not an option. Too expensive."

"Tough break."

We sat in tense silence until Shirley returned with my breakfast. The white ceramic plate was piled high with fluffy pancakes smothered in whipped cream and candied pecans, with a generous portion of bacon that was just shy of being burned. I swallowed a bite over the lump forming in my throat. It tasted like home, and I smiled up at her. "Oh, I've dreamed about these."

Shirley swirled her ballpoint pen in the air in front of me before nestling it behind her ear. "This one's on the house. We missed you around here, girl. Although I didn't expect a dead body on your first day back in town."

"Not my doing, I promise," I said loudly enough for the half of the restaurant that was already eavesdropping on our conversation to hear.

She wiped a spot off the table with a white rag and tucked it into the front of her apron. "Oh, I know that. Doris Sadler had a king-sized line of people who wouldn't have minded drop-kicking her into the grave. Her killer probably had to take a number."

My fork clanked on the ceramic plate, and I whipped my head up to meet Shirley's gaze. "Who else is on that list?" I asked, digging through my purse for a pen.

"You didn't hear it from me, but that snooty assistant of hers came in here for a dozen frosted crullers the night Doris died." Shirley glanced over her shoulder and leaned in close, giving an exaggerated shudder. "She's an egg white omelet, extra spinach, kind of woman, so it was odd to begin with."

I stuffed a syrup-coated slice of bacon into my mouth and raised a brow, saying a silent prayer of thanks for carbs and talkative neighbors.

"She started cramming those things in her yapper like she was getting paid for it," Shirley continued. "She was so jumpy and wild-eyed that crumbs were flying everywhere. She was like a donut woodchipper."

I snorted at the visual, then quickly covered my mouth with the napkin to hide my grin.

"I tried to ask her about it, but she got a phone call and

bolted out of here like her hair extensions were on fire. Didn't even leave a tip." She grabbed an empty glass off the table and stuck out a finger. "Something was definitely off with her that night."

"Interesting," I said, scribbling a note on the napkin.

Ian's gaze narrowed as he studied me across the table. "What are you doing, Glory?"

I flashed him a grin. "Beverlee is tied up in knots about Doris's death, and since I can't afford a fancy wedding gift, I'm giving her the next best thing: a killer."

9

I met Beverlee and Edwin at her house after lunch. I slumped down in the zebra print wing back chair across from them and shook my head. "No, we don't have time to train parrots to recite your vows on your behalf."

Beverlee patted Edwin's hand and gave him a shy smile. "I think we're both nervous we will forget our lines."

"Relax," I said. "This isn't a school play. Just talk to each other from the heart."

Edwin brought Beverlee's hand to his lips. "I don't want to mess it up. The first time I got married, I was so nervous I almost threw up all over the bride."

My eyes widened in alarm. "No gastrointestinal pyrotechnics this time, okay, Edwin? If you get nervous, picture your guests in their underwear."

He wiggled his brows. "Guests without pants. Got it."

"You've told me you're looking for something unique. Because you've both been married before, we can move past some parts of a more conventional ceremony." I consulted my notes. "Edwin, tell me what you picture when you imagine seeing Beverlee at the altar. Are there any images that pop out at you?"

"If I have to picture the guests in their skivvies, I vote for that visual to carry over to the bride."

Beverlee swatted him on the arm. "We don't want it to be too serious. Everything we have planned so far is about color and adventure."

"Hence the pirate theme," I said, digging through my purse for headache medicine.

"Exactly," Beverlee replied. "The bigger, the better."

"Go big or go home." I half-heartedly pumped my fist in the air. "Have you chosen a song for your first dance?"

Edwin shook his head. "I don't dance, I'm afraid. Two left feet."

"Not even at your own wedding? Can't you just pick a song and sway?" The whooshing of blood in my ears made it hard to focus. "Never mind, where do we stand on the appetizers?"

"We finalized the menu a few weeks ago," Edwin said. "My sweet Beverlee is a wizard when it comes to food. You should taste her latest creation. It's a seafood bisque that will have people up and down the coast beating down her door for the recipe. She's going to be a star."

Beverlee blushed. "I like to feed the people I love."

"My waistline and I thank you." He rubbed his stomach.

Beverlee described the feast she had planned for the reception. "We'll have local seafood dishes, of course, along with a selection of Eastern North Carolina produce. But the centerpiece will be the knife buffet."

I choked on my own laughter. "Excuse me?"

"Kebabs," Beverlee responded with a sigh. "We will have a table dedicated to food on tiny knives. Seared filet mignon with mushrooms and pearl onions. Roast pork medallions with smoked poblanos. Mahi-mahi with fresh pineapple chunks."

"Sounds delicious, but what's with the food on weapons?"

"Not weapons, baby. Skewers. We won't be having utensils."

I looked at her in alarm. "Your wedding planner couldn't get you silverware for your wedding?" Forks were one thing I knew I could do.

"We asked her not to. Beverlee suggested we should eat with our hands to bring us closer to nature... and each other." Edwin rubbed his thumb over his fiancée's back. "And I agreed."

I pinched the bridge of my nose. No forks. Got it. "Can we at least have napkins?"

Beverlee glared at me. "We're not heathens, Glory."

"Of course not," I said, but I wasn't so sure.

"There's something else I'd like to talk to you about." Beverlee leaned forward, the corner of a beaded throw pillow cradled between her palms. "I need your help with a special wedding detail."

I felt a wave of panic.

Beverlee fidgeted with the beads and avoided making eye contact. "This isn't my first wedding. But it doesn't make it any less important to me."

"I know," I said and took a deep breath. "I'm here to help. What can I do to help make it the best one yet?"

Her gaze softened. "Your mama was not only my sister, she was also my best friend. During the good times and the bad, we were inseparable. From the first moment I saw her, she was my baby." She stopped and took a sip of tea from a delicate porcelain cup on the side table, her hands trembling. "That never changed, not for a single moment of her life."

I felt a lump form in my throat. We didn't talk about my

parents much when I was growing up. I always imagined it was because Beverlee didn't want to upset me, but maybe it was the other way around.

Beverlee gripped my hand, her eyes glistening. "I see her in you. The way you throw your head back when you laugh and the wrinkle you get between your brows when you're trying not to insult somebody. The way trouble seems to follow you around no matter what you do to avoid it. That's all her."

She placed her teacup back on the table and focused out the window. When she finally spoke, her voice was quiet and wistful. "When somebody you love dies, you're left with this person-sized hole in your world. And no matter how many other people you try to fit into that hole, they never quite match. We want to honor the people we've lost." She looked at Edwin for a long moment, then turned back toward me. "I realize being here is hard for you. There are a lot of memories in this town, some of them no doubt hard to see face-to-face."

I thought of Ian but couldn't bring myself to respond.

Beverlee continued. "But having you around has been so nice. With you back in Flat Falls, that hole that your mama left doesn't seem so big anymore. In fact, it seems almost Glory-sized." She squeezed my hand. "I guess what I'm trying to say is that I'm glad you're here."

I closed my fingers around hers. "Me, too."

She picked up her napkin and dabbed at the corners of her eyes. "So, you'll do it?"

I squinted at her in confusion. "Do what?"

"Be my matron of honor. The only other time I had a bridesmaid was the first time I got married. Your mama was my maid of honor then. It seems only fitting for her only daughter to take her place this go-round."

I smiled and sighed with relief. That wasn't so bad. I could do that. "I'd be honored."

Beverlee grinned and raised her teacup in a toast. "Fantastic. You girls will look beautiful."

I raised a brow. "Girls? I thought you said it was just me."

"Just you and Matilda, dear. A woman over in Beaufort traded me my famous funeral bread recipe for a vintage gilded birdcage. It's gorgeous. You can carry it down the aisle instead of a bouquet."

I groaned. I was about to become the only woman in history to escort a bedazzled chicken down the aisle.

FOLLOWING the visit at her house, Beverlee and I stopped at the bridal salon for her last dress fitting.

The only dress shop in Flat Falls was an upscale boutique that boasted ample windows with direct ocean views and price tags to match. Wall-to-wall racks of wedding gowns looked like streams of marshmallow fluff against textured black wallpaper. Crystal chandeliers glistened above elevated platforms surrounded by mirrors.

Beverlee insisted I wait in the lounge area so I could get the full effect of her gown. I had just settled onto a pale pink sofa and flipped open a bridal magazine when I heard a voice drifting down the hall from the other fitting area. "It's awful, but I don't think anybody will figure it out. We were careful. "

The voice halted as a woman entered the room talking into her cell phone. Dressed in a floral shift dress with light blue wedge sandals and a matching statement necklace, her light brown hair pulled back in a low ponytail, she appeared fresh-faced and polished. "I've got to go. I'll call you back," she said, before hitting a button on her phone and dropping it into her handbag. She turned toward me with a smile. "Glory? Is that you?"

I stood and raised my hand in a wave at Ian's younger sister, Kate Strickland, who I hadn't seen since before I had left Flat Falls the first time. "In the flesh."

She trudged across the room and gave me a half-hearted hug. "I heard you were back in town." Her tone had grown cool, and I added her to my mental list of people who weren't happy I was back.

I nodded. "Just for a week or so until Beverlee's wedding."

Her stiff smile didn't meet her eyes. "I've met Edwin a few times down at the bar. Nice guy."

The salesperson chose that moment to fling open the curtained area with a flourish. "I am happy to present the future Mrs. Edwin Calhoun."

My aunt, a woman who I thought of as a mother and loved with my whole being, twirled around on a little platform looking like a pirate wench who'd pillaged a plus-size lingerie department. The dress was bright red with little bits of white lace accentuating areas that didn't need to be accentuated. Black satin ribbons embellished with black buttons crossed the bodice to make it into a bustier. Her cleavage spilled over the top like it was making a march for freedom.

"Ta-da!" Beverlee threw her arms wide, and I ducked my head quickly, worried one of those buttons would come shooting off and blind me. "What do you think?"

I looked over at Kate, whose mouth had dropped open.

"Wow," I said.

Kate's head was bobbing up and down. "Yes, wow."

Beverlee seemed to take our stunned silence as a compliment. She stepped off the platform and sashayed across the room, her large skirt swishing behind her. She did a quick twirl and stopped with her right hip thrust out to the side. "They special-ordered it just for me. Isn't it spectacular?"

Thankfully, she kept talking so I didn't have to answer. "Kate, are you here for your last fitting, too?"

Kate smiled in return and pointed down the hall toward the other fitting room. "Yes, we're getting all finished up."

An emerald-cut solitaire diamond glittered from the top of her left hand. "I didn't know you were getting married. Congratulations. Anyone I know?"

Before she could respond, Beverlee pushed between us. "She's got herself quite a catch. Isn't that right, Kate?"

Kate held out her finger to show off the ring, a flashy monstrosity that reflected more light than an airport strobe. "Dex Harvey and I are getting married in a few weeks. Do you remember him from school?"

I flashed on a picture of our star quarterback, a womanizing jock who brought every high school athletic legend stereotype to life. I couldn't very well say *Yeah, I remember. He got drunk at Homecoming and tried to make himself at home in my B cup. When's the big day?*

"I remember. Broad shoulders, big brown eyes? Went to some Ivy League school after graduation?"

Beverlee's head bobbed up and down, her cleavage bouncing like it was made of deflated whipped cream. "That's him. Came back home from Columbia a few years ago to take over his daddy's real estate business and fell in love with Kate here. They make quite a handsome pair."

I forced a polite smile. "Congratulations. How romantic."

Beverlee continued. "He's responsible for turning all that abandoned property along the waterfront into fancy new townhouses. Very highbrow." Beverlee shimmied, and I jerked my head toward Kate in alarm. "He will be running for the NC Senate next year. It's an exciting time for our little town."

"You must be so proud," I said, pressing my fingernails into my forearm to keep from rolling my eyes.

She lowered her lashes. "He has a servant's heart."

Gag.

Beverlee bobbed on her heels and clapped, her dress sliding dangerously lower with each jiggle. "Young love. So beautiful."

Kate averted her gaze from Beverlee's inadvertent peep show. "Yes, well, I didn't expect to run into trouble this late in the planning process," she said.

Beverlee patted Kate's arm. "What kind of trouble are you having, dear?"

"Doris was planning everything." Kate crossed her arms across her chest. "With the tragedy, I am feeling out of sorts."

"Yes, it's terrible. Unimaginable." Beverlee sighed and turned back toward the mirror. "We were just in to see Magnolia ourselves earlier. Have you checked with her about your wedding plans? I'm sure she can help you sort things out."

Kate nodded. "Yes, she's going to handle everything. She said she would take over all of Doris's weddings, so she didn't leave any clients in the lurch. She showed up at my house with a bottle of champagne and a folder stuffed with paperwork like some sort of wedding angel."

I scowled and looked away from the mirror, where Beverlee appeared to either be practicing her dance moves or trying to wriggle out of her underwear without using her hands. I turned toward Kate with renewed interest. "She had all of your documents? Where did she get them?"

Kate shrugged. "Dex has a contact in the police department. When they heard how upset I was about the disruption in our plans, he made a copy of everything they took from her office and sent it over. We'll be scrambling to get through it all in time, but at least we're not starting from scratch."

Beverlee murmured in agreement. "That is good news. You should give us a call if we can help you. You know Glory is a wedding planner, right?"

"I'm not a wedding—" I protested, but Beverlee clicked her tongue, and I shut my mouth. "Happy to help," I said through a clenched jaw.

Beverlee turned with a loud swish. "We've got to run, dear. Keep us posted." She took my hand and dragged me toward the dressing room. Once we had gotten out of earshot, she snapped the curtain shut and yanked on the corset ties. "Help me get out of this thing."

I pulled once, releasing the ribbons, and Beverlee took a deep breath that sounded like a big truck's air brakes, then leaned in with a whisper. "Hear that, Glory? Maggie had Kate's wedding paperwork, so don't you think it's strange mine has disappeared?"

"Wedding files don't just disappear," I replied, nodding in agreement. "There's got to be a reason yours weren't in the office. If we find those files, I'll bet we have a better idea who killed Doris Sadler."

10

After the dress fitting, we drove by Doris's house to see if we could find the missing files. Instead of a neon sign in front of the well-kept bungalow telling us where to look for clues, we found Hollis Goodnight sitting on the street in his police car. Beverlee slowed to a stop behind the car and lowered the mirror to touch up her lipstick.

"What now? We can't just waltz in and check out a dead woman's house," I said with a nervous glance at Hollis's cruiser.

"We are friends of the deceased. It would be downright indecent of us to not come by to pay our respects." Beverlee smacked her lips together and opened the car door. When I didn't move, she leaned back into the driver's side and raised an eyebrow. "Are you coming or not?"

I looked toward the ignition. She had taken the keys, and the Carolina summer sun was already turning the car into a rolling air fryer. I didn't relish the idea of roasting to death like a pork chop while she freshened her makeup, so I sighed and popped open the passenger door. "Fine."

I followed as she sauntered up to the sedan. When she

made it to the driver's side door, she cocked one hip out and pushed her sunglasses to the top of her head. Hollis rolled down the window.

Beverlee smiled and stuck a hand inside, coming out with a barbecue potato chip from the bag on the chief's lap. "Doc Willis told you to cut out the chips."

"He also told me to get rid of the stress in my life, yet here you are." I heard the crinkle of the bag as he shoved the chips down in the console. Hollis studied Beverlee with practiced restraint. "Can I assume you're not here to check my cholesterol?"

Beverlee reached through the window and put a hand on his shoulder, flashing a quick look down toward his lap. "Don't be silly. We both know you're healthy as a horse."

I cleared my throat and peered around Beverlee. "We're glad you're here, Chief. We've been trying to find the official paperwork for Beverlee's wedding. Magnolia said it wasn't at the office, so we were hoping your team might have already picked it up."

Hollis pushed his car door open, nudging Beverlee out of the way. "The women in your family are something, aren't they? Trouble, the lot of you." He stepped out into the sun and pulled his hat lower over his brow. "I don't recall seeing anything with your name on it, but I'll be sure to let you know once we release Ms. Sadler's effects."

Beverlee batted her lids a few times. I'm sure she thought it was flirty, but she looked like she had a bug caught in her false lashes. "We don't have time for that, Hollis."

"Can we take a quick peek inside to see if they're on her kitchen table?" I asked.

"No can do, ladies," Hollis said. "We haven't cleared the house yet. I'm waiting on the crime scene team to get finished up at the boat. Then they're headed over here. Nobody's allowed in until they're done."

She pursed her lips. "It's just a few files, Hollis. I can't plan my wedding without them. And you are aware of how important this day is."

Hollis seemed to consider her request for a few moments before shaking his head. "I hate to throw a wrench into your plans, but I can't let you in there. And besides, those files might be evidence."

"What kind of evidence?" I asked.

"You were one of the last people to see her alive, Beverlee," Hollis said. "And she was killed in the middle of planning your wedding. It's clear that anything having to do with the two of you will be of interest in the investigation."

Beverlee huffed and crossed her arms, shooting the chief an annoyed glare. "Hollis Goodnight, you know I had nothing to do with that horrid woman's death."

"It might help your case if you stopped calling her names," I whispered to Beverlee. She had always been known for sticking her high heels in her mouth, but this time she was flirting with getting both of us arrested.

She brushed me off with a swat. "Well, she was. She was mean, spiteful, and had terrible taste in table linens. But that doesn't mean I killed her."

The crackling of Hollis's radio signaled his team's arrival. A uniformed officer came toward us and spoke with him in hushed tones.

With a short curse, he turned back to us. "Turns out the investigative team can't make it out here this evening due to engine issues." He stuffed the radio back into his pocket. "And I have enough going on without worrying the two of you are off causing trouble. Can you go home and let me do my job?"

Beverlee nodded enthusiastically. She leaned forward and gave Hollis a quick hug. "Of course. It was lovely to see you, as always, Hollis. You'll have to come over for supper once this is all taken care of. I'll make your favorite. Pot roast and mashed turnips, right?"

Hollis patted his stomach and ambled toward the house.

Beverlee marched back down the sidewalk, her high-heeled sandals clicking on the pavement. She sighed in defeat. "What are we going to do now?"

I took a deep breath. Beverlee had done everything for me, and I owed her at least a little larceny in return. "We'll wait until they all go home tonight. Then we'll come back and get what we need."

～

LATER THAT EVENING, as we hid in the bushes outside Doris's house, I wondered how my life had come to this.

Six months ago, I had been living my dream. I had a great job, great friends, and what I thought was a decent husband. But like dominoes, they fell away one by one.

I didn't realize how much my life would change after Cobb left. I went from planning the biggest events in the city, surrounded by sequined friends and chilled champagne, to being single, friendless, and broke, all within a few days.

"Let's scoot around to the back. Less chance for a looky-loo to drive by and spot us," Beverlee whispered. She slid out from behind the hedge, brushed a stray leaf off the front of her catsuit, then dashed around to the back of the house.

I rolled my eyes and followed her.

As I rounded the back corner of the house, I peeked in the kitchen window. Because the rear of the cottage faced away from the street and toward the water, Doris hadn't bothered covering her kitchen window with curtains. The moonlight cutting through the windows gave me an unob-structed view of the space.

The kitchen was mostly white with stainless steel appliances. It looked clean, and there weren't any dishes piled up in the sink.

I had left a tall stack of cereal bowls sitting in my sink back home before I left town. How embarrassing if I ended up dead and somebody had to come in and clean my counters or pick up the laundry scattered on the floor like a textile-based obstacle course.

I made a mental note to tidy up as soon as I got home. You never knew when there would be strangers traipsing through your breakfast nook.

"Bingo!" Beverlee exclaimed, her fingers wiggling under a terra-cotta planter of flowers near the back door. She extracted a key and held it up to the light in triumph. "It's not breaking and entering if we have a key, is it?"

No sooner had I begun pondering her question than I heard a loud creak and spied Beverlee pushing the cottage door open. She glanced back over her shoulder and raised a brow. "Are you coming, or do I need to have your invitation engraved?"

Beverlee pulled two small flashlights out of the bosom of her catsuit and handed one to me. I stared at it for a moment and wondered what else she had in there.

"Let's split up," I said. "No point in us being here any longer than we have to."

I started down the hall and realized I was heading for the bedrooms. I passed a small guest bathroom, so I stopped in there first, closing the door behind me and clicking on the flashlight.

White subway tile lined the floor, and light peach towels embroidered with shells blended into the cream walls. Not my style, but pleasant enough. I started to pull open a drawer but realized I should leave as few fingerprints as possible, so I quickly cleaned them off with my sleeve. I hooked my knuckle under the drawer pull and used it to slide the drawer the rest of the way open.

Grabbing a cotton swab out of a box on the counter, I used it to move things around in the cabinet, proud of myself for not leaving a trace of my presence.

Aside from a few old *US Weekly* magazines, a nail file, and a travel-sized container of plum-scented hand sanitizer, the drawer was empty. I nudged it closed with my knee.

I used the same procedure to open the cabinet under the sink. The only things under there were a plunger and a six-pack of toilet paper. She bought the expensive stuff. Triple-ply. I made another mental note to splurge on better toilet paper the next time I found myself flush with cash. Life was too short for the scratchy stuff, especially if people would judge me if they had to search my house to solve a murder.

There wasn't anything else noteworthy in the bathroom, so I grabbed a fluffy handful of toilet paper and covered the knob before I opened it. Then I was left standing there with a wad of evidence. I reached over to the toilet and dropped it in, flushing with my foot before I rushed out of the room.

Beverlee appeared outside the bathroom. "I told you to pee before we left the house."

"I wasn't—"

She waved me away. "I haven't found anything yet. What about you?"

I shook my head and then headed further down the hall. "I'll check her room next."

In the moonlight shining through the window, Doris Sadler's bedroom looked like the rest of her house. Everything was pristine and eerily perfect. From the crisp, folded blanket resting across the foot of the bed to the perfectly aligned classic books on her nightstand, everything was in its place. I fought the impulse to muss up the straight row of khaki throw pillows along the headboard.

With a tap of my finger, I flicked on the flashlight and ran it around the room. My hopes to find a manila folder labeled "Beverlee's Wedding" lying on a table were dashed. There was nothing related to her business at all.

I nudged open the dresser drawers one by one but didn't see anything out of the ordinary except one bright red lacy negligee folded neatly atop a pile of cream-colored slips.

I flipped open a small wooden jewelry box. A pair of pearl earrings and a matching necklace were tucked into a navy velvet bag. A few costume brooches were nestled into lined compartments, a burgundy velvet pouch held a single gold band, and a handful of small gray rocks and several gold studs were spread out along the bottom of the drawer. Even her jewelry was drab.

"Find anything?" Beverlee asked from behind me, which made me jump and drop the flashlight, leaving us engulfed in darkness.

"It's a pantsuit wonderland in here," I replied, pointing to the closet. I bent down to retrieve my flashlight and shook it to get the light to come back on. "Not much else, though."

"Come help me in the living room. It appears Ms. Sadler was quite the collector."

I shuddered. What kind of collection would a rigid middle-aged woman living alone have? Cats were too easy. Maybe leather ball gags or bloody throwing stars or Mason jars full of toenail clippings. I secretly hoped Doris had an outrageous fetish. Otherwise, her beige and boring life made me more than a little sad.

We stepped into the living room and I was vaguely disappointed to see there weren't any velvet-lined cases containing tiny pieces of taxidermy. Instead, it looked just like her bedroom. There were white couches with navy nautical pillows. A small television sat on a wooden stand across the room. A book on beach photography and a few wedding magazines were lined up along the coffee table.

"What is so interesting out here? Looks just as boring as the rest of her house."

Beverlee pointed her flashlight up to a painting on the wall. "For being so understated with the rest of her house, Doris seems to have interesting taste in art, don't you think?"

I inspected the painting and noticed it was a full male nude, painted with his back toward the artist. His flexed muscles, enhanced by deep, dark strokes, made him look sexy and dangerous. I ran my knuckle along the surface of the man's upper back and could feel the ridges of dried paint. It was almost life-sized and definitely an original. "Oh my. Nicely done, Doris." I turned to Beverlee. "I was beginning to think she was an automaton."

Beverlee moved her flashlight around the room, highlighting at least half a dozen more paintings, all of which appeared to be by the same artist. Beverlee shined her flashlight in the corner where ten more canvases were propped against the wall. "I'm looking for more of the guy." She laughed and fanned herself. "I wouldn't have pegged Doris for a collector of fine male specimens like that."

A flash of relief tore through me. A woman couldn't live a life this repressed without having some sort of outlet. "Who knew? Beige Doris had a wild side."

Just then, a loud creak sounded from the back of the house. Both of us spun toward the kitchen, and Beverlee clicked off her flashlight. She put her finger in front of her lips and pointed at the front door.

We heard the click, click of heels across the kitchen tile and dashed toward the exit, but the door had a keyed deadbolt. I motioned for Beverlee to hand it to me.

"I left it on the counter," she whispered.

Click. Click. The woman's footsteps sounded like a timer, slow and steady.

I grabbed Beverlee by the hand and yanked her into the bathroom, shutting the door behind us with a soft tug. I tried to quiet my breath, but my heart was drumming in my chest with such force, I was sure even the people down the street could hear it.

Click. Click.

Beverlee looked at me, her eyes wide. *What do we do?* she mouthed.

I raised both hands in question. "How am I supposed to know?" I whispered.

A closet door opened and closed with a snap.

The shrill ringing of a phone from the hallway made both of us jump.

The mystery visitor picked up on the first ring. "What? I'm working on it. You don't have to keep checking on me. I'll call you as soon as I have them."

Her voice was low and quiet but held a condescending Southern twang I knew well. What was Maggie Winters doing in Doris's house?

We stood frozen in the bathroom and listened to more doors slamming and drawers opening and closing. I peeked over at Beverlee, her face illuminated by a thin stream of moonlight shining through the window. She released a dramatic sigh. Maggie obviously wasn't concerned with burglary etiquette or she would be quieter.

After a few minutes, her footsteps retreated. The back door creaked open and then clicked shut again. "What do we do now?" Beverlee asked.

I lowered my voice. "We wait for a few minutes to make sure she's long gone, then we get out of here."

She nodded, then sat down on the closed toilet lid, her

foot tapping a quiet rhythm on the bathroom floor. "That girl is up to something," she whispered in reply.

I chuckled and lowered my voice. "She was skulking through a dead woman's house. 'Up to something' might be a bit of an understatement."

The clock slowed while Beverlee scratched an invisible stain off the bathroom counter with her fingernail. Patience never had been part of her skill set.

Finally, she sprang up in a huff. "I can't wait any longer." She threw open the bathroom door, and barged right into Maggie, who was standing in the hallway, high heels dangling from her fingertips.

"Well, look what the muskrat dragged in," she said, her teeth flashing white in the darkness. "I should have known you two would be up to no good."

Beverlee pushed past her into the hallway, wiggling her fingers in the air inches from Maggie's face. "It's lovely to see you, too, Magnolia."

Beverlee started to walk away, but Maggie grabbed her arm before she could get far. "You're not going anywhere," she said, her glare darting back and forth between me and Beverlee. "You have no business here. I should call the police."

I slipped between them and tugged Beverlee's arm free. "Go ahead. I'd be interested in hearing you explain what you're doing here, too."

Maggie laughed. "I was her assistant. I'm doing my job. It's perfectly reasonable for me to be here."

I pointed toward the back door. "So that shiny yellow tape across the doors that says, 'Do Not Cross' applies to everyone but you?"

She looked back and forth between Beverlee and me for a moment before speaking. "Fine." She sighed. "I was looking for something Doris was keeping for me. Something private."

"Paperwork that shows your mail-order Russian boyfriend has finally come through?"

She glared and stepped toward me, her eyes flashing, and fists clenched at her sides.

Beverlee cleared her throat, then smiled. "So, what is it you're looking for, dear? Maybe we can help you find it."

Maggie shouldered past Beverlee and made her way back to the kitchen. "It's nothing."

As the three of us entered the kitchen, we passed by a small desk built into the cabinets. A white lacquer tray filled with a single manila folder had been pushed into the far corner.

Maggie and I glimpsed it at the same moment.

We both dove for the folder and, in a quick tangle of limbs and ponytails, tried to grab it at the same time. I snatched it out of the tray first, but then Maggie grabbed the other side.

We faced off, neither of us willing to concede. My stomach muscles tensed as the nervous seconds passed. We stared at each other, nostrils flaring and two decades-worth of hostility simmering just underneath the surface.

"Let go," she said between gritted teeth. "It's mine."

"I don't think so." I snarled back and pulled. "I saw it first."

Maggie was several inches taller than me, but I had her in width. I reared back and hip-checked her, knocking her to the side and coming out victorious.

I held out the folder to Beverlee like a trophy. It could have contained Doris's grocery list or her most recent colonoscopy results and I wouldn't have cared.

I won.

Beverlee nodded. "That's my girl. Now let's get out of—"

With a feral screech, Maggie launched herself across the room and threw her full weight into me. We both tumbled to the ground, along with the folder's contents. Papers fanned out around the room.

Not a grocery list. A collection of pictures and printouts featuring Beverlee and Edwin were spread around the floor. A snapshot of Beverlee at the market. A recipe for dill pickle tartar sauce printed from her blog. A hand-sketched layout of Bill Judson's boat.

"At least she did her research," I said, and started gathering the papers.

Maggie pushed herself up from the ground and gave me one last glare before storming out the door into the balmy night.

11

I returned from my adventure with Beverlee to find Josie watering the plants on her balcony. I squinted up at her and waved.

"Nice hat," she called down the stairs. "Why does it look like you just robbed a bank?"

I remembered the black cap I was wearing and slid it off. I shifted nervously and looked around, half expecting to see flashing squad car lights in the alley behind me. "What? No. What?"

She disappeared inside her apartment and met me at her door. Her voice was a whisper as she glanced over my shoulder. "Please tell me you didn't rob a bank, Glory."

An awkward giggle slipped out before I could stop it. "Not a bank, exactly."

She grabbed my arm and pulled me into her apartment, then shut the door quickly behind us. "What have you done?"

I didn't want to confess to a crime, but I needed to talk through what happened. I studied the ankle monitor strapped to her leg. She wouldn't run to the cops, so I plopped down on her sofa with a sigh. "We might have broken into Doris Sadler's house tonight."

"The dead lady?" she said with a lifted brow. "Impressive."

"Yes. If Beverlee isn't cleared of this murder, then she's going to jail. So, we went looking for the missing paperwork to see if we could piece some of this puzzle together, or at least find the details she needs to pull off this wedding at the last minute."

"Did you find anything?"

"We found a file full of pictures and information about Beverlee, but not much else."

"And you don't think that's weird?" she asked, narrowing her gaze.

"Not really. I always researched my clients before an event. You can find out a lot about a person by stalking them on social media. You'd be surprised how fast somebody will hire you when you show up with a drink from their favorite coffee place or a bouquet of their favorite color of tulips."

Josie walked to the refrigerator and came back with two cans of soda. She popped the top and handed me one. "True. But I still think it's creepy."

I took a sip. "We found something else that was interesting, though. Doris had a thing for art. Sexy art."

"Nice." She raised her soda in a toast to Doris. "People have all sorts of weird collections. I once knew a man who collected ancient burial artifacts. He had a skull, a real human skull, on his desk at work."

"Gross."

"Everybody has a dark side," Josie said. "And you said it yourself— we can find out about Doris by cyberstalking her."

"Okay, I'll Google her tonight and let you know what I find."

She snorted. "If you want to find out where she goes to church, sure. But if you want to find pictures of that time she got arrested for throwing her khaki bra at her college algebra professor, you need to dig deeper."

I leaned forward, more than a little awed by my new friend and her over-the-top skill set. "And how do I do that?"

She sighed and stared at me for a few seconds before responding. "Bring me your laptop. If I'm going to get nosy, I'm doing it under your login."

JOSIE'S FINGERS flew across the keyboard for nearly an hour. Every few minutes, she got up and paced around the room, brows furrowed in concentration. She mumbled, picked at the fuzz on her sweater, and stared at a blank wall for minutes at a time.

"Find anything?" I asked, tapping my foot on the floor.

She held up a finger. A moment later, she turned to me with a frown. "It's weird. I can't find anything about the woman before she showed up in Flat Falls five years ago. Nothing. That's not normal."

"Beige Doris didn't strike me as the secretive type. Her makeup was even alphabetized."

"Secrets are like Amazon wish lists. Everybody's got at least one."

"Maybe she doesn't have a history for a reason. Maybe she was in Flat Falls hiding out from somebody."

"Something like witness protection? I'll look into it," she said with a quick nod before returning to her keyboard.

My stomach lurched at the thought that she was using my computer to skulk around in places we probably shouldn't be searching. I laid a warning hand on her shoulder. "Isn't this illegal? Are you sure you know what you're doing?"

Josie sat back on the sofa and kicked her foot onto the coffee table with a loud clunk. She pointed at the ankle monitor. "See this? How do you think somebody would go about getting one of these beauties?"

I shrugged. "I can't imagine."

"You get one of these when you're the head of computer security for one of the largest banks in the world." Her voice rose, and her spine straightened with every word. "You get one of these when you're the best at following people down their rabbit holes. The holes where they hide their crazy."

I nodded slowly, afraid to make any sudden moves so Josie didn't pull out her own inner psycho and lay it across the coffee table next to my feet.

"You get one of *these*," she said, "when you're so busy falling in love with somebody you fail to notice they're using you to funnel cash out of that same business."

She slammed the lid of the laptop closed. "You do not get one of these for not knowing what you're doing."

I held out both of my hands and took several steps backward. "Understood."

She cleared her throat. "So, what was Doris hiding? And who killed her for it?"

"From what I hear, the list of people who hated Doris was a long one. Beverlee fought with her at the diner, so she's definitely on it."

Josie nodded. "But is Beverlee a murderer?"

I tapped the pen against my chin. "Not a chance. If she doesn't like you, she sends you a Bless Your Heart cake and writes you out of her life."

She turned to me with wide eyes. "She gives people cakes to tell them she hates them?"

"Yes. Devil's food." I smiled. "She's not subtle. She once spent three solid days baking red velvet cupcakes for the church choir because somebody told her the crimson robe clashed with her lipstick."

I grinned at the memory. Beverlee was a passive-aggressive baker, but those cupcakes were delicious.

"If it wasn't Beverlee, then who else is there?" Josie asked.

We talked through the rest of the suspects. Maggie Winters was shady, but she was more likely to bore people to death with her stale personality than to actually knock them off. "As much as I despise Maggie, I can't see her going after her boss. But what was she looking for in Doris's house? You don't just break into somebody's house in the middle of the night."

Josie gave me a pointed stare.

I waved her away. "We had a good reason."

"Perhaps Maggie did, too."

I considered that for a moment, then nodded in agreement. "I need to find out why she was there."

"And what about Ian's sister, Kate? You said she had a secret, too."

I chewed on my lip. "She was hiding something, for sure. But even if Doris suggested an aisle runner made of decapitated unicorns and worm guts, I can't see her committing murder over it."

"Planning a wedding can be stressful."

I remembered the itemized list Beverlee handed me that morning and groaned. "Tell me about it."

I took another sip before I leaned back against the sofa cushions. "The obvious choice is Bill Judson," I said. "He's a cranky old man, but I have a hard time picturing him as a murderer."

"Her body was found on his boat," Josie pointed out.

"But he and Doris didn't even meet each other until a few days ago."

Josie nodded. "You need to ask around about him. There are enough busybodies in this town. Somebody should know if he's capable of murder."

12

I tried finding information at the Grind and Go, but my second visit was as unproductive as the first.

I thought I was getting somewhere when Ginny Thomas, who used to cut my hair when I was a teenager, offered me a seat at her table. But as soon as I sat down, the curious glances and hushed conversations started. Ginny noticed, too, because she left half of her lemon poppy seed muffin on the table and rushed out the door for a last minute "hair emergency."

People had started whispering. It seemed like everywhere I went, there was a sideways look or a murmur of disapproval. And it wasn't just about me. Instead of rallying behind Beverlee, the social calls had slowed down. I was used to being on the outside looking in, but the view was new to Beverlee, and I could tell by the dark circles under her eyes that it was wearing on her, too.

It looked like I was on my own.

After a slow stroll back toward the apartment, I sat on the steps out front. I had only been out there for a few minutes when Rusty bounded up and dropped his ball at my feet. When I wound my fingers through his soft fur, an idea crept into my head.

I knocked on Josie's door. When she answered, I nodded down toward Rusty. "I'm going to take him for a walk."

She nodded slowly, narrowing her gaze like she wondered if I had lost my mind. "Thanks for telling me."

"No. I'm going to take him," I said with a pointed stare. "We're going to go for a walk. Down by the boats."

Her eyes got wide. "Oh, I see. You're snooping and you needed a wingman."

I grinned. "Do you have a leash?"

She raised a brow. "What would I be doing with a leash, Glory? It's not like I can go on waterfront tours every afternoon with my invisible Pomeranian."

I flushed and stumbled to apologize. "I'm sorry, I wasn't—"

With a sweeping motion of her hand, she invited me inside. "I'm kidding. I don't have a leash, but I think I have a piece of rope that will work."

She fumbled through a closet until she pulled out a piece of rope about six feet long. She tied a knot around one end, looping it through Rusty's collar, and handed me the other end. "Have a good time storming the island, you two."

I wrapped the rope around my hand and headed off down the boardwalk toward Old Bill's boat. I needed an excuse to poke around down there, and nobody questions a dog walker.

Rusty trotted along beside me, his tennis ball clenched between his teeth. Now and then, I lingered for him to eye an errant seagull or sniff a trash can.

As we made our way down to the end of the public dock and into the more isolated area at the end of the island, the air became thicker. Gnats buzzed around my face. In the shadows of gnarled live oak trees, the walkway was dotted with gray moss and stray pieces of driftwood. I couldn't feel the sea breeze as well under the canopy of branches, and a drop of sweat slid between my shoulder blades.

I made it to the end of the street where Old Bill's boat was moored. I made a show of holding Rusty's leash, so in case anyone was looking, it would appear I was enjoying a blazing hot stroll with my dog, who had eyed me with suspicion once he realized we weren't stopping to play fetch anytime soon.

There didn't seem to be anyone else around. Old Bill's rusty orange pickup truck was gone, as was the blue bicycle he kept against the side of the wooden gear box on the dock. Whenever he drove into town, he would throw the bike in the back. Then when he got too drunk in town, he'd have an easy ride home and wouldn't have to deal with the police.

I assumed he had gone into town for the day, but I walked the length of the boat and called out, "Hello? Anyone there?"

No response except for the gentle lapping of waves against the seawall.

I was about to climb aboard when I heard the distant crunch of tires on gravel. I tightened my grip on Rusty's leash and yanked him behind the dumpster that sat on the other side of the lot.

Heat radiated off the metal in waves that smelled like three-day-old shrimp and dirty dishwater. Rusty's body wriggled next to me. "Be still," I urged him, "and I'll get you all the rotten seafood you want before I take you home."

He plunked to the ground, tail still wagging.

I peeked around the edge of the dumpster. A man stood near the water, his arms crossed. He was tall and tanned, his hair an inky black. Mirrored sunglasses hid his eyes as he surveyed the area around the boat.

A few minutes after he arrived, Old Bill's pickup truck

came barreling down the street with the sharp grinding of metal on metal and a plume of gray exhaust.

I jerked behind the dumpster just as he got out and advanced toward the other man. Once Bill had passed the dumpster, I felt safe peeking out again. This time, I had my phone in hand. With my hands shaking, I pulled up the camera and took a picture.

Old Bill's voice was loud and booming. "About time you made an appearance."

The other man looked around. "There's too much heat around here. Did you take care of our little problem?"

Bill nodded. "Done. Shouldn't be any more questions, but I'm prepared if there are. I drove into town this morning to make sure everything was rock solid. Even if the police come sniffing around, they won't be able to pin anything on us."

Sunglasses Man shifted back on his feet and crossed his broad arms across his chest. "See that there's no trouble. We have too much riding on this to let some know-it-all podunk police chief screw it all up." He nodded toward the boat. "Can you provide me with an assurance that everything is going according to plan? I'll need to report back on your status. People are getting nervous."

Old Bill pumped his head up and down. "Of course, of course. Follow me. Everything you're looking for is well-secured below deck."

They had started to make their way toward the boat when a seagull caught Rusty's eye. He let out an excited series of barks.

Both men turned toward the dumpster. The stranger pulled his sunglasses down and stared straight toward me. "What was that?"

Old Bill turned and stepped across the clearing. "Probably just a stray."

My stomach dropped and a wave of nausea crashed over me. I had no choice but to release the leash from Rusty's collar. I hoped Ian would forgive me for getting his dog killed.

Rusty took off like a bullet, unaware that he was chasing a seagull straight into the path of a murderer.

He bounced across the clearing with single-minded focus until he remembered the two people standing there. Given his penchant for doggy optimism, he must assume one of those people might have a treat hidden in his pocket, so he trotted right up to them and dropped his ball between their feet before plopping down in a perfect sit.

Neither man seemed amused. Old Bill sighed gruffly. "Never seen you down this far before, mutt."

Sunglasses Man reached down and grabbed Rusty by the collar. I couldn't let that sweet pup suffer the same fate as Doris Sadler. I swallowed my anxiety, mussed my hair, and ran out from behind the dumpster. Nerves and a lack of exercise for the better part of the last five years already had me breathing hard. "There you are, you silly boy. I've been looking everywhere."

Rusty's tail thumped as I walked toward him, and he rolled over to expose his belly, apparently unaware it's bad form to ask for tummy rubs from a killer.

I quickly tied the rope around Rusty's collar. "Hey, Bill, hope we didn't disrupt your obviously important business."

I grimaced. Nervousness bubbled in my vocal cords and made me babble even more. "Great weather today, huh? Not a cloud in the sky. Super breezy when you're down on the—"

Old Bill stopped me by raising his wrinkled hand in the air and lowering his voice. "You best be getting your dog back to town now, girl."

"Yes, I'll do that. I'm sure you have important things to do." I nodded like my head was attached to a spring, and I couldn't figure out how to stop the bobbing. "Thanks for helping me with Rusty. I appreciate it." I gave them an exaggerated wave and turned back toward the road. "Enjoy your day."

I pulled Rusty along beside me and it wasn't until I made it all the way out to the main road that I got up the nerve to look back over my shoulder. Both men were still standing there, arms crossed, watching me. Sunglasses Man had pulled the frames down his nose and his hard stare gave me chills even despite the late summer heat.

13

I made my way back toward Ian's boat, surprised to find him sitting on deck with a cup of coffee. I reached my hand down to release the knot from Rusty's collar, my hands still shaking from the scene outside Old Bill's boat.

"Back so soon? Josie told me you had kidnapped my dog. I figured someone would call me in a few hours to bail you out of jail. I didn't think you were actually taking him for a walk."

The jab didn't even register. I tried to smile, but it came out like a hiccup, followed closely by a sniffle. Ian was up in an instant, hopping over the side of the boat and onto the dock. "What is it? What happened?"

I wrapped my arms around my waist to warm myself up, but it was useless. I still trembled. "Ian, I figured out who killed Doris."

Ian lifted a brow. "Must have been some kind of walk."

"I'm serious, Ian." I took in a shaky breath. "And he might know that I know." As the tears fell, Ian wrapped his arm around me and gently guided me to a nearby bench.

"Why don't you start from the beginning? I'm eager to

discover how you solved a murder before the police, who have been working around the clock since it happened."

"It was Old Bill." I sniffed. "He killed Doris right there on his boat."

Ian snickered. "Old Bill? The same guy who used to dress up like Santa Claus for the Christmas parade until he got too big for the suit?"

"Yes, I—"

Ian put his hand on his chest like he was trying to stop himself from laughing. "The same person who donated all new uniforms to the football team our senior year after that kid was smoking in the locker rooms and set the whole place on fire? That guy?"

I sighed. "Ian, you've got to—"

He wiped a tear from the corner of his eye. "That's a good one, Glory. Old Bill's a fixture around here. No way he's your murderer."

My shoulders slumped, and Ian narrowed his eyes. "Wait, you're serious."

"I'm afraid so," I whispered, stuffing my hands into my pockets to stop them from quivering.

He sat back on the bench and folded his arms across his chest. "Tell me what you think you saw."

I told Ian about the meeting between the two men. I told him about scary Sunglasses Man and how Old Bill told him that he took care of the problem. "He took care of it, Ian." My voice rose in both pitch and volume as I spoke. "His problem was Doris Sadler."

He stared at me for a minute and then dipped his chin. "There's got to be another explanation, but I agree that what you saw suggests otherwise. We need to call Chief Goodnight."

HOLLIS DIDN'T BELIEVE ME, either. He chuckled, his belly shaking underneath the tan uniform shirt that was already strained at the buttons from too much diner food. "Let me get this straight. You were eavesdropping on the man and, with absolutely no context, decided he confessed to murder? You're talking about Old Bill, Glory."

"Yes, but—"

"That man has been a part of this community for seventy-five years. Heck, did you know there was a motion put forward at the town council meeting last year to name the new post office after him?" Hollis hooked his thumb through his belt loop and nodded toward his office window, beyond which stood the town's municipal complex. "Yes, he's gruff, and probably scares small children. But you don't get a building named after you if you're a murderer."

I sighed in defeat. "You weren't there, Hollis. The man he met with gave me the creeps, and the whole meeting was sketchy."

His burgundy leather office chair made a groaning sound as he leaned back. He crossed his arms behind his head. "Honey, I understand you're trying to help get your aunt out of the heap of trouble she's found herself in, but you're looking in the wrong direction. I haven't heard anything that makes me think Bill Judson has done anything wrong."

I stood up to leave, then remembered the picture I had taken of the two men when I had been behind the dumpster. I sat back down and emptied my overstuffed purse onto the edge of his desk. His eyes got wider as I pulled out a parking ticket, two tubes of lip balm, a tampon, and a half-eaten bag of peanuts.

He watched in amusement until I found my phone and laid it in front of him. "I knew it was in there." My phone's lavender glitter case looked odd against the austere mahogany of his desk.

I tapped on the phone. "I have proof they were having a weird meeting. Old Bill and some dark-haired guy in sunglasses and all black. He had on long sleeves and long pants in the middle of summer. Nobody does that." I picked up the phone and pushed the power button, but my battery was dead.

"Bad fashion choices don't make someone a criminal. Otherwise, I'd have to arrest half this town." Hollis stood and motioned toward the door. "Why don't you send it to me when you've got it all together? Someone will check into it."

"Hollis, he's the murderer. You need to listen."

He took a deep breath and exhaled slowly, much the same way that he did when I was a teenager and sitting across this same desk from him explaining why my aunt's car had ended up fender-deep in the marsh across the bridge when I was supposed to be at a friend's house studying for a history test.

"I can see that you're serious, Glory. But I've known Bill Judson for over thirty years. He's harmless. Can't handle his whiskey anywhere near appropriately for a man his age, but he's not a killer. I'll tell you what, though," Hollis said as he patted my shoulder on his way to the door, "I'll ask him tonight at our weekly poker game and confirm it for you."

14

I waited until late afternoon before visiting Beverlee.

I found her in her back garden, a large straw hat covering her head. She was digging around in the dirt with a trowel. Matilda was pecking at the ground next to her.

I raised my hand in a greeting. "What are you planting?" I asked.

Over the years, Beverlee had filled her garden with everything from vegetables to medicinal plants. Most recently, she had tried her hand at growing wormwood because she had been dating an older man who had an eye patch and fancied himself a trendier version of Ernest Hemingway. She thought she would make him a batch of homemade absinthe.

Unfortunately, the old man met his sea mistress and ran off with a truck stop waitress before the plant bloomed, so she ripped it out and the earth had been barren ever since.

"Oh, I'm not planting, dear." She continued running her fingers through the soil. "I'm making a charcuterie board for Matilda's dinner." She nodded over toward her worn picnic table, where a rustic slab of maple sat piled high with corn and carrots and fresh berries.

I remembered I hadn't eaten and thought about stealing a snack until Beverlee squealed with delight and plucked an earthworm from the ground and deposited it, still squirming, in the center of the board. She then put it on the ground in front of Matilda and gave the chicken's back a gentle stroke before standing and brushing the dirt off her hands.

"Can I make you a bite to eat, too?" she asked.

I studied Matilda, who was chowing down on her chicken buffet with clucks of pleasure, then shook my head. "Worms aren't my thing, Beverlee."

"You might be surprised. They're high in protein." She wiggled her eyebrows. "Some cultures even consider them an aphrodisiac. In fact, I might need to grab a container for my honeymoon."

My stomach wobbled. "Remind me to never travel with you."

She put her hand on my back and pushed me toward the house. "You're in luck. How about I make you a toasted pimento cheese and tomato sandwich and you tell me why you're here looking like somebody just ran over your prized thorn bushes?"

Beverlee refused to call them rose bushes because she said it's not the thorn's fault. It's just the way it was made.

Beverlee's pimento cheese was legendary, so my reluctance to have a snack was quickly drowned out by the growling of my stomach. "I guess I could eat."

I sat in the high-back chair at her kitchen table while she washed her hands and puttered around the room. It was her happy place. If she could feed you, there was hope for you yet.

As she buttered a slice of homemade sourdough bread, she looked back over her shoulder. "I wasn't expecting you this evening, but I'm glad you stopped by. Edwin is working, and it turns out your social calendar clears right up when everybody in town thinks you killed someone. The whole town went from wanting to devour the details of Doris's murder to throwing the sign of the cross at me when I walk by."

Her tone was flippant, but there was sadness in her slumped shoulders. Beverlee could handle a lot of things in life but being ostracized wasn't one of them.

I hesitated for a moment. "I came by because I needed to talk to you about something."

Beverlee flipped the bread and turned around, pointing at me with the tip of her spatula. Butter hissed in the pan, and the smell of melting cheese permeated through the room. "Man trouble? Because I heard you and Ian have been putting off enough sparks to send the space shuttle into orbit."

"It's not Ian," I replied. "I think I know who killed Doris Sadler."

She turned off the stove and plated my sandwich, then placed it on the table in front of me. "And who is that, dear?"

I swallowed, and my mouth felt like it was filled with sawdust. "It was Old Bill."

Beverlee flashed her trademark I-told-you-so smirk. "What makes you so sure?"

I recounted the events of the day, and Beverlee leaned against the counter and listened patiently. When I finished my story, she sighed. "It does sound like he was up to no good. We need to get more information so Hollis will take me off the suspect list."

With a quick jerk of my head, I responded. "Hollis knows you didn't do it."

"Does he?" she asked. "This morning, he invited me down to the station, and when I got there, he sat me in a room and asked me all sorts of questions about my relationship with Doris Sadler. He didn't even offer me coffee or a pack of crackers."

My jaw dropped open. "He officially questioned you about the murder?"

Beverlee slumped down into the chair next to me. "What happens if they think I'm guilty? Will Edwin still want to marry me if I'll be spending our honeymoon in jail instead of on a tropical island?"

I squeezed her hand. "Of course he'll want to marry you. He adores you."

She huffed. "And even if he does want to go through with it, how is that going to work? I cannot get married if people are convinced I am a murderer, Glory. People don't come to the weddings of killers. I have a five-course meal planned for two hundred people who won't attend if they think I have turned into the Flat Falls Slayer." Her voice turned shrill. "Do you want to be responsible for that many servings of uneaten tiramisu?"

I sighed. "No."

"Then how can we prove I'm innocent?"

I drummed my fingers on the table and stared out the sliding glass door, watching Matilda bask in the sun after her snack. "Old Bill will be tied up at the poker game for a few hours tonight," I said slowly. "So maybe we should visit the boat to see if the police missed anything."

Beverlee nodded, her hair bouncing with enthusiasm. "We'll consider it part of our wedding planning."

"Yeah, sure. Because most brides want to have their ceremonies at a crime scene." I shuddered, flashing back to the image of Doris Sadler's dangling corpse.

"There's a first time for everything," she said as she headed back toward her bedroom. "But I haven't washed yesterday's breaking and entering clothes yet. Come back in an hour. It should give me plenty of time to round up backup and do a quick wash of my catsuit."

WHEN I RETURNED to Beverlee's house an hour later, I found her in the kitchen wearing a slate-colored romper and bright red high-heeled sandals. "I thought we were planning to sneak, Beverlee. That's not an outfit meant to fly under the radar."

She thrust out a hip. "Under the radar's not my thing. Besides, Edwin's taking me out for drinks after our adventure. I needed an outfit that could multitask."

I heard a snicker and turned to see Scoots huddled over an iPad at the table.

"Oh, great, the gang's all here," I said, dropping my bag onto the counter.

Scoots pointed down at the screen. "We're looking for egress routes in case things go south with the investigation."

"We live on an island. There's no way to go except back the same way we started."

Scoots ignored me and tapped the screen. "Bill's only got one neighbor. It's a boat owned by some doctor out of Raleigh. He doesn't usually come down here in the summer on account of the mosquitoes and his wife's unwillingness to show her pasty legs in a bathing suit. It'll be locked up tight." She snickered again. "Like his wife."

She turned and looked out the window. "There's some moonlight out there tonight, so you'd be visible on deck. There's only one other option if you get into trouble and need to make a quick escape." She pointed at the satellite map on the tablet. "There is a dumpster at the end of the street next to Old Bill's boat."

I nodded, remembering the stench of rotting fish. "I'm familiar with it."

"There's a bunch of old oak trees in a group behind the dumpster," Scoots continued. "It's pretty overgrown and marshy in there since the last hurricane threw up so much debris, but there used to be a path that led down to the house."

Beverlee sashayed into the room, fastening large rhinestone earrings to her ears. "I wouldn't exactly call it a house, though. It's not much more than a fishing shack with cable and a creaky old double bed."

"How do you know what kind of bed he has in there?" I asked, not sure I wanted to hear the answer.

Beverlee smiled and blinked several times.

Scoots huffed and then made a show of pulling a retractable hunting knife out of the pocket of her overalls. She flicked open the blade and inspected it under the kitchen lights. Then she pointed the blade toward me like an extension of her finger. "Get back on track, girl. You need to be prepared for the unexpected tonight."

I shuddered. I wasn't prepared, and that was one of the problems. The other? It looked like I was about to become a criminal... again.

15

We drove my Honda because it was the only discreet car we had. Beverlee's mustard yellow Volkswagen convertible was meant for splashy summer days, not nights of crime.

I glanced over and saw her, pursed lips inches from the side mirror, sweeping on a shade of lipstick so red it looked like she had dipped her mouth in candied apple syrup. She tucked the tube into her cleavage and grinned.

Everybody climbed in the car and I pushed the button to let in some air, trying not to wince at the windows' protesting groans as they struggled to make it all the way down.

"Can't we turn on the air conditioner like normal burglars?" Scoots asked.

I swiped my forearm across my brow to keep the sweat from dripping into my eyes. "We could if it worked."

Fixing the air conditioner hadn't been a priority after Cobb left. Instead, I spent my money where it mattered, like on rent and Starbucks.

I looked in the rearview mirror to find Scoots flushed

and fanning herself with a crumpled-up supermarket flier from the floor. "It's like a rolling hot flash back here," she said. "Your car makes me cranky and sweaty in my nether bits."

I put the car into drive and pressed the gas. Awesome. Nothing started a crime spree better than a discussion of post-menopausal lady parts. "Stick your head out and you'll get more air."

She leaned her head out the window and her cheeks flapped in the breeze. The wind pushed her crepe paper skin toward her hairline, giving her an instant face-lift.

Beverlee had tied a bright pink floral scarf around her head before we left and seemed untouched by the heat. As we approached the dock, she leaned over and put her hand on my arm. "Slow down for the approach, honey. We want to look like we're out for an evening drive, not like we're casing the place."

I slowed the car and parked under the darkness of a group of live oak trees a short distance up the road from the small marina. As soon as I cut the headlights, a hush fell over the car.

Scoots spoke first. "Leave your keys here in case things go sideways."

"Let's do this," Beverlee said, untying the scarf and placing it neatly in the passenger seat. Her cheeks were flushed, and her eyes sparked with excitement. She seemed to be enjoying our second venture into the illegal arts more than was appropriate. She climbed out of the car and headed toward the boat, darting between trees and gesturing for us to follow her.

A combination of nervousness and dread tugged at my belly, but I dropped my head and dutifully followed her down the road. Gravel and oyster shells crunched beneath my feet with each step, the noise echoing off the water nearby.

When we reached the boat, I leaned in toward Beverlee and whispered, "How do we know he's gone?"

"Old Bill hasn't missed a poker game in years. Trust me, he's gone."

When she climbed aboard, though, she called out a friendly greeting. "Bill? Anyone home?"

No response.

Beverlee motioned for me to follow her. I climbed over the railing and the boat dipped under my weight. We left Scoots to be our lookout from the dock.

The boat was every bit as ghoulish as I remembered, its shadows in stark contrast to the moonlight. It pulled against its lines with each wave, and I felt the accusation in each creak. Several strips of yellow crime scene tape had come loose and slapped against the deck in the breeze. Somebody had cleaned up the body, but even bleach couldn't cover up the overwhelming stench of mildew and rotting teak.

My stomach threatened to revolt as I remembered the wedding planner dangling from the mast a few feet away. I pointed at Beverlee. "I can't believe you wanted to get married here."

She brushed me off with the wave of a hand. "You have no vision."

"But I do, that's the problem. I don't see string lights and a harpist. I see a creepy boat where a lady died. There's my vision."

Beverlee huffed and pointed toward the stern. "Harpist there." Then she swept her hand along the railing near where we were standing. "White folding chairs here. Lights around the mast. Open your mind. Visualize."

I squinted. I still couldn't visualize anything but a crime scene.

Scoots called from the side of the boat. "Don't mean to rush you along, but can we stick to the plan?"

"Good idea." I looked over my shoulder at Scoots. "What are we looking for, anyway?"

"Anything that looks out of place. Anything that will connect Bill to the murder."

I followed Beverlee as she peeked under tarps and lifted buckets. The only things out of the ordinary were a candy bar wrapper and an angry lizard.

I eyed the hatch door and shuddered. "This happens in every horror movie I have ever seen. The girl does something stupid like go below deck by herself on a murder boat, only to have the killer find her and chop her into bits with his chain saw."

"Don't be so dramatic, Glory. We're right here," Beverlee said, her bangle bracelets jingling as she gestured toward Scoots. "And there are no chain saws in sight."

"Watch my back, I'm going under." I stepped over to the hatch for a closer inspection. "Bad news. It's locked."

Beverlee followed me across the deck and reached into the pocket of her jumpsuit and pulled out a bobby pin. "No problem," she said, as she stepped between me and the lock.

"Did they teach you that in blogging school?"

She winked. "I am a woman of many skills, Glory. Lock-picking, however, is not one of them."

"Then how did you—"

She twisted a section of her hair and secured it back with the pin. She leaned over and gave the lock a sharp tug. "Bill can't keep up with his keys. He always pushes the padlock until it's almost closed but doesn't lock it all the way. It deters casual observers and those people who don't have the fortitude to follow through on things."

I ignored her pointed stare. "And you know this intimate detail about Old Bill how?"

She raised a brow and motioned to the hatch.

I pushed past her and slid back the top panel. "Follow through on keeping an eye on things while I go below."

She patted her silver hair. "Whatever you say, dear."

I stepped down into the main salon of the boat and scanned the room. There were stacks of magazines and newspapers everywhere, and any surface not buried under piles of paper was littered with take-out boxes and empty cans of RC cola and cheap beer. Plastic bags full of more papers lined the floor around the dinette and a single overstuffed recliner sat crammed against the far wall, covered with a brown and orange crocheted blanket. An ancient television topped with a twisted metal coat hanger balanced haphazardly on two milk crates in the corner.

It looked like the home of a serial killer who had a serious hoarding problem.

I flipped through a few pieces of junk mail in the galley kitchen's small sink. I pulled out a dog-eared lingerie catalog and fought a wave of queasiness. Old Bill liked them racy, it seemed. "Not here to judge," I muttered, slipping the catalog back into the stack.

I moved toward the aft sleeping cabin. It was V-shaped, with single beds lining both walls and coming together at an angle. The mattresses were compressed under the weight of about a dozen cardboard shipping boxes. I pulled a box down and gently pried open the top, barely suppressing a shout of relief when I flipped it open and found food instead of severed body parts.

Beverlee's heels clicked as she walked on the deck above me. A few moments later, she popped her head in through the hatch. "Find anything interesting down there?"

"No, but Old Bill must like hush puppies. He has a bunch of boxes of cornmeal mix down here."

"Grab one of them and let's go."

My jaw dropped. "You want me to steal his food?"

"I do like a good seafood boil," Beverlee replied.

I rolled my eyes and grabbed a box from the top, shuffling the remaining boxes to fill the empty space. I pushed the box in front of me as I climbed the steps to the deck. When I got to the top, I thrust it toward Beverlee. "Here's your snack."

She took the box and carefully tossed it over the side of the boat to Scoots, then climbed over the rail to the dock below.

I closed the hatch and followed her.

We were almost to the car when Beverlee cursed and fished the padlock from the front of her jumpsuit. "I forgot to put this back on."

We all stared at the lock. Scoots looked down at her watch and shook her head. "It's late. There's no time to return it."

"We have to," I said. "Otherwise, he'll know we were there."

Beverlee nodded so hard I expected her teeth to fly out of her mouth. "It's true. He always could tell when I'd paid him a visit."

I wasn't sure whether to be impressed or appalled. "How many visits are we talking here, Beverlee?"

She didn't respond.

"Never mind." I grabbed the lock from her open palm and shoved it into my pocket. "I'll go back. You two wait in the car."

I turned back toward the boat, each step filling me with a greater sense of dread.

I had just slipped the hasp back into place when I heard the telltale crunch of tires on gravel. "Oh no," I muttered. I was running out of time before Bill got back.

After leaping from the side of the boat onto the dock, I

made a quick run for the dumpster. But instead of Bill's rusted truck, a dark sedan came to a stop in the clearing. Sunglasses Man stepped out of the car, and I could tell from his scowl he wasn't delivering flowers.

I lost sight of him when he boarded the boat, but the crack of wood splintering as he broke the boat's hatch reverberated like a gunshot along my already frayed nerves.

Looking down the road, I tried to calculate my chances of making it back to the car without being seen, but the sight of my Honda's taillights disappearing told me I was on my own.

I peeked back around the dumpster. Sunglasses Man had brought out one of the boxes from Bill's boat. It was sitting on the ground next to his car.

Go on, I thought. *Take your box and go.*

He wasn't in a hurry to leave. Instead, he loaded the box into the trunk and leaned back against the hood. He lit a cigarette. Then he smoked it. While checking his phone.

I sighed and slid into a crouching position, shifting so I could smack a mosquito that had landed on my thigh. The rotting fish smell was making me gag, and I wanted nothing more than to get home and curl up with an ice cream sandwich and some itch cream.

Another mosquito buzzed around my ear, and I shook my head to keep it from biting me. If I ended up in a coffin after this stunt, the last thing I wanted everybody staring at during my viewing was a puffy pink welt on my cheek. I must have moved too quickly, though, because Sunglasses Man whipped around and glared toward the dumpster. He dropped the cigarette butt and ground it into the gravel with his boot and advanced toward me.

As he stepped closer, I looked around for an escape. My only choice was the overgrown path Beverlee had told me about. I pushed my way through the brush and took off at a sprint.

Darkness enveloped me and briers grabbed my clothes and knotted in my hair. The thick brush felt like a thousand tiny knives slicing into my skin as I ran.

Faster. Harder.

His curses echoed through the woods as he followed me through the thick foliage.

Blood trickled down my cheek and into my mouth. Sweat blurred my vision and drenched my clothes. The night air swirled around me and fear threatened to choke the air from my lungs.

I stumbled over a fallen branch, slamming into the ground with a thwack. The tang of copper hit my lips and I wasn't sure if it was from me or the damp earth. I brushed the back of my hand across my lips and clawed my way through the debris until I finally made it to the clearing.

Old Bill's house was little more than a wilting garden shed with a single window on one side.

It wasn't a fortress, but it was my only chance.

I ran toward the door, almost shouting with relief when the weathered brass knob turned beneath my shaking fingers.

I threw the door open and rushed inside, closing it quickly behind me and flicking the deadbolt from the inside. I pressed my back to the cold metal as I caught my breath and took in the surrounding room.

My eyes had adjusted to the darkness, and I could barely make out a small table and a little kitchenette. The double bed Beverlee promised took up a large portion of the remaining floor space. And sprawled across the middle of it was Old Bill Judson, eyes wide open and a thick, red slice across the front of his battered throat.

My head started to spin. "Mr. Judson," I whispered as I leaned over and nudged his arm.

His body slumped back on the bed, his head clunking into the wall behind him.

Just then, I heard the rattle of the door and the crunch of leaves as heavy-booted feet stomped around the shack.

The windows didn't have curtains, so there was nowhere to hide. Sunglasses Man was going to find me. And he would kill me, too.

I dove across the room and squished myself next to the bed frame, pulling Old Bill's musty orange and brown crocheted blanket across me to shield me from view.

I tried to slow my breath so the blanket didn't move, but it smelled like mothballs and cigar smoke, and the loose threads scratched like sandpaper on my skin.

The door handle rattled. The window shook in its frame, and I issued silent thanks when it stayed firmly closed.

A flashlight shone on the window, and spots of light peeked through the tiny holes in between the blanket's stitches. Bill's waxy arm dangled off the bed next to me.

I wanted to scream. I wanted to run.

Instead, I held my breath, my pulse ricocheting around my body.

Seconds passed, then minutes. I didn't dare to inhale, certain that even the tiniest movement would lead him to find me. And if he found me, there was no way for me to escape.

The light from the flashlight disappeared and the window shook as Sunglasses Man tried to open it. He muttered a curse when the lock held.

It was only a matter of time before my luck ran out. Old Bill's shack wasn't Fort Knox, and it wouldn't be hard for a killer to find his way inside.

With careful movements, I poked the top of my head out from underneath the blanket and scanned the room for a possible weapon. Defending myself would be a challenge unless I could figure out how to repurpose the fishing pole tucked away in the corner or the half-empty wine bottle on the bedside table.

A horn honked in the distance, and I wasn't sure if it was from a boat or a car. But whatever it was, it made Sunglasses Man abandon his post right outside the window.

I took my first deep breath as he moved away from the cabin, shells crunching under the weight of his heavy boots.

A full-body shudder jolted my body as I slid out from under the covers. I glared at the man reclined so casually on the bed next to me. "Oh, Bill," I whispered. "What did you get yourself into?"

The horn blared again, followed by the screech of tires right outside the building. At the sound of a car door slamming, I dove back toward the bed. I had just pulled the blanket back over my face when a whispered drawl broke through the silence. "Glory, honey, are you in there?"

I choked out a sob. It was Beverlee. The cavalry had arrived.

I threw off the blanket and lurched toward the door, thumbing the lock and taking in a deep, shaky breath as I fought the darkness threatening to overtake me. "Beverlee," I said, stumbling into the clearing. "He's dead. Old Bill has been murdered."

16

"Let me get this straight." Gage leaned back in his desk chair and tapped his pen on the desk, the stark fluorescent lights in his office buzzing overhead. "You found another dead body."

I stifled a sigh. "I had nothing to do with it."

His slow nod told me he didn't quite believe me. "Want to tell me why you were in the victim's private residence, then?"

Frustration came on quick and strong, like the zap from an electrical outlet. I forced myself to stay seated and took a moment to slow my breathing before I spoke again. "Like I told you, there was something weird going on. There was this guy…"

He squinted at the notes he had scribbled on the pad of paper in front of him. "Sunglasses Man."

"Yes, Sunglasses Man was on Old Bill's boat." I shifted back and forth in my seat. "What was he doing there?"

"A better question might be what were you doing there?"

"I told you, I was looking at the boat for Beverlee's

wedding. As her wedding planner, it's my job." I crossed my arms and pursed my lips, daring him to argue with me.

"Beverlee is one of the prime suspects in an ongoing murder investigation, Glory. She needs to be more worried about staying out of trouble than planning a party if she doesn't want to spend the rest of her life behind bars."

I looked at him in alarm. They still thought she did it. I pictured my sweet aunt, the woman who had raised me as her own child and fought back a swell of tears. "Gage, you know she is innocent."

He leaned forward and spoke slowly. "If you want her to stay out of jail, you need to tell me the truth. If you weren't there to cause trouble, why did you run?"

"The guy gave me the creeps, okay? They teach us early in Girl 101 classes to not stick around if someone sets off your weirdo alarm." I raised a brow. "Are you saying I should have stayed there so I could be the next victim? Or have you forgotten there's a killer on the loose?"

Irritation flashed across his face, and he pointed at the papers strewn across his desk. "No, I haven't forgotten."

"What are you doing about it?" I asked, desperation triggering a series of thudding heartbeats low in my chest. "I'm practically gift wrapping a suspect for you."

"Fine." He loosened his tie and rolled his shoulders, then bent his neck to the side, the loud crack like a pencil breaking in half. "Tell me about this guy. Tell me about Sunglasses Man."

Reaching into my purse, I flashed him a smile. "How about I do you one better? I'll send you a picture."

I STOOD in the shower that evening until the water ran cold, but I still couldn't wash the image of Old Bill out of my head. My stomach turned every time I thought about his weathered face and grumpy attitude. How he was up and growling at me just the day before, but now he was gone.

Steam blanketed the bathroom mirror when I finally stepped out from underneath the shower spray, but the warm air swirling around me was no match for the goose bumps peppering my skin. I tugged on a fluffy white hotel robe, a remnant from a long-ago romantic vacation before my husband turned into a thief and I started finding dead bodies, and made my way to the kitchen to start some water for a cup of something hot and soothing.

After rummaging through the cabinets for a tea bag and coming up empty-handed, I slumped against the counter. A sharp knock at the door made me jump, and I banged my head against the cabinet.

I shuffled to the door, muttering curses under my breath as I rubbed the back of my skull and peeked through the peephole. Hollis Goodnight stood on the other side, his tan police hat gripped in front of his chest. I debated not opening the door, but he said, "Open up, Glory. I know you're in there. You're a loud breather."

My fingers tightened on the doorknob. I took a steadying breath and swung the door open. "What does a girl need to do to get some peace around here?"

He lifted a paper bag from his side and held it out. "Gage told me you had a rough night, so I brought you a muffin and some hot chocolate. I thought you might have been too tired to stop and eat."

The bag crinkled as I snatched it from his hand and stuck my nose down in the top. The scent of cinnamon and cloves hit first, transporting me back many years to the first time I'd had one of the café's pumpkin spice muffins. Hollis had been bringing me these for years, especially when I'd found myself in trouble. "You remembered," I said, opening the door to allow him to come into the apartment.

He nodded once and stared at the ground. "It's my job to remember things."

I smiled and popped a piece of the top of the muffin into my mouth and took a slow sip from the paper take-out cup he offered. "Well, thank you. It's the best thing I've eaten in a while."

He patted his stomach. "I find that hard to believe, given what a good cook Beverlee is. You mean to tell me she hasn't been over here, feeding you three square meals a day?"

I laughed. "She's been a little distracted these days."

He shoved his hands into his pockets with a grunt.

"So, aside from delivering me the world's best pumpkin muffin, to what do I owe this visit, Chief?"

He hiked his gun belt up and cocked his head to one side. "I know you've been away for a while, but Flat Falls is a sleepy little town. That's why people like it here. It's almost the end of the summer and the tourists are heading out, which means I get to spend the winter fishing and occasionally dealing with lost dogs and domestic disturbances from fishermen who are spending too much time at home annoying their wives."

I nodded and took another bite of muffin.

"But now I've got two bodies in less than a week," he said. "That's two more bodies than this town has had in the last ten years."

I sank onto the sofa, gesturing for him to take a seat in one of the chairs. "I know. It's odd, isn't it?"

"Look, Glory, I'm not going to beat around the bush here. Several people in my office find it suspicious that all of this activity started when you came back into town."

I straightened. "What are you saying, Hollis? Do you think I had something to do with the murders?"

He made a patting motion with his hand. "Settle down. I'm just saying it's awfully coincidental. That's one of the reasons I wanted to stop by here tonight, so we could go through any recent events in your life that might have followed you back home."

I snorted. "First of all, this isn't my home anymore."

Hollis sighed. "You've been gone a while, Glory, but this will always be your home. The place where you can come when you forget who you are or where you're going. Where people love you because of your history—or in spite of it. That's what home is."

My heart hitched in my chest. I hadn't thought of Flat Falls as home in years. But I had felt a sense of nostalgia when I drove through town, a sense of belonging more here than I had anywhere else.

I swallowed the last bite of muffin, then balled up the brown paper bag, rising to throw it out so I could put space between the two of us. His line of questioning was getting uncomfortable, and I wasn't ready to tackle my personal history with this town.

"I'm aware of the surface stuff. Beverlee shows me your Insta-whatever photos every chance she gets."

"Instagram."

He brushed me off with a wave. "Whatever. You're into throwing fancy parties and taking ridiculous pictures of them."

"It's my job," I said. "Well, it *was* my job." My cheeks flushed, and I turned away from him before he could notice the shame on my face. I wasn't quick enough, though, because he stood and followed me into the kitchen.

"I never got a chance to tell you how sorry I was about that no-good husband of yours. How long has it been since you've gotten word from him? He hasn't been bothering you since you got back, has he?"

I looked over my shoulder. "You seriously believe he has something to do with this? He's a liar and a cheat, for sure, but he's not your guy, Hollis."

"Just covering all of my bases here. Can you indulge an old man?"

"You might be many things, Chief, but I wouldn't ever call you old." I nodded at the gun attached to his hip. "Because you might shoot me if I did."

He patted his belt and smiled. "Haven't fired this thing off the range in a while. May need to take it for a spin, though. Where's your husband now?"

"Ex-husband. Or at least he will be soon." I pictured the paperwork I had paid a lot of money having my lawyer assemble. "But, no. I haven't heard from him since he left. I guess he didn't need anything once he humiliated me and stole my money."

Hollis nodded, his eyes narrowing into menacing slits. "And I assume you filed a police report?"

"I tried. But we were married, and the law says it was his money, too."

"I hear he left you in quite a pickle at one of your fancy shindigs."

"If by pickle you mean that he meandered off with the cash box at the most important event of my career, then yes. He left me in a pickle."

"Why didn't you file charges?"

"My client didn't want the bad press associated with her event," I said. "And neither did I. It's not good for business."

"So, you paid your client back for what your husband stole."

"Ex-husband," I reminded him. "And yes."

"How did you do that? I remember Beverlee telling me you had put every penny you had into starting your company."

"I sold things. A lot of things."

"But you don't think Cobb would hold a grudge? Something that would make him follow you here?"

"He ruined me. He trashed my reputation and stole my money. I can't imagine what kind of grudge he'd have against me, though. I'm afraid the grudges are all one-sided and aimed toward him."

He nodded, the side of his mouth turning upward. "Want me to find him for you?"

I laughed until I realized he was serious. "You could do that?"

He tapped the badge on his chest. "Seems like you have a valid complaint, baby girl. I get that you just want to move on with your life, but if you don't file charges, the scumbag wins. And I can't just sit by and let a scumbag win. I've got to protect my people."

A feeling of warmth settled in my chest, but it disappeared quickly when I looked up and saw his grin vanish.

"That's the other reason I'm here, Glory," he said, his voice somber. "I can't protect your aunt if I don't know what's going on."

Panic shot through me like he had filled the room with ice water. "Is Beverlee okay?"

"It depends," he replied. "Remember the shack where you found Bill Judson's body?"

The muffin threatened to make a surprise reappearance, but I nodded slowly.

"I've known Bill for decades, and I can explain almost everything in that place. I recognized each piece of fishing tackle and the old street sign he pulled from the dump when they dozed the marina. Even the old blanket he bought at the Christmas Bazaar," he said, leaning toward me with a steely gaze. "But there's one thing I had no explanation for. Can you tell me why the whole crime scene was peppered with Beverlee's fingerprints?"

17

I was still reeling from Old Bill's death, but not even the dreary day or a second murder could put a damper on Beverlee's wedding plans. She showed up at my door the next morning with a cup of coffee and a mile-long to-do list, starting with a wedding cake breakfast.

Before we headed out, I told her about the evidence Hollis had found in the shack.

"Bill and I were friends," she said, waving her hand in the air like the whole idea was nonsense.

I pinched the bridge of my nose. "Then why didn't he want you to use his boat?"

"He was a private man, and he didn't want a bunch of strangers loose on his private property."

"But why—?"

"I don't want to talk about other men, Glory. It's disrespectful to Edwin," she said firmly. "And speaking of Edwin, we have a whole day of wedding preparations. Let's stop dwelling on the past and concentrate on my special day."

Arguing with Beverlee was futile, so I kept my mouth shut and pulled out her color-coded schedule.

We spent the morning zigzagging across Flat Falls and when we finally made it to the holy land, I took a deep breath and sighed. Nothing cheered a girl up faster than the smell of baked goods.

From pillowy white balloon valances over the windows to glossy yellow melamine tables flanking a glass display case filled with pastries and petit fours, Flat Falls Cakery was a confection all by itself.

I sat down across from Beverlee and watched as she opened her giant purple tote bag and pulled out several pieces of photography equipment and a variety of props, including candles, delicate lace doilies, and a small plastic bag brimming with heart-shaped silver confetti, which she scattered across the tabletop. "I thought this was a cake testing. What's with the portable hobby store?"

Beverlee cocked her head to the side and studied me. "You need a brighter shade of lipstick for this. I can't have my wedding planner looking washed out for her blog debut."

"My what?" I asked, realizing not even dessert would make up for what was about to happen. "I don't want to be on your blog, Aunt Beverlee."

She patted my hand. "Don't be silly. Of course you do." She busied herself with setting up a tripod and arranging fake white tulips in a cluster on the table. "Edwin and I have already picked out the flavors for the actual cake, but I'm writing a blog series about the wedding and the bakery was more than happy to give us a second tasting so I can get some pictures. A little free press never hurt anybody, especially if it goes viral."

That's what I was afraid of. The last thing I needed these days was to go viral. I had enough trouble getting the media to leave me alone after the scandal with Cobb. I certainly didn't want any of them following me here and digging up my old dirt.

"It's your day, and I have an idea," I said, my voice falsely cheerful. "How about I take the photos? Your readers don't want to see me on such a special day. They want to see you. You enjoying your cake, you making plans. It's all about you." I jabbed my finger onto the table in emphasis.

She stuck a hand back in her bag and came out holding a shutter release remote, then waved it in the air like a trophy and tucked it into the front of her shirt. "You're such a sweet girl to think of me, but now we can both be in the pictures. I wouldn't have it any other way."

I bit the inside of my lip so hard I was afraid I might draw blood. I didn't want to disappoint her, and at least I was getting cake out of the deal. So, I pasted on a smile. "Wonderful."

She grinned and gestured to the woman standing behind the counter who had prepared two silver trays filled with a variety of cakes, fillings, and frostings, along with tall glasses of champagne. "We're all set. Let's get this party started."

As the late morning turned into early afternoon, Beverlee didn't show any signs of slowing down. She was still stuffing spoonfuls of frosting and bites of cake into her mouth, taking notes, and snapping pictures, and she had asked for frosting refills twice.

She finally pointed at me with a spoon filled with lemon curd. "This is the life, isn't it? I could stay here all day with you, eating the goodies and watching the clouds over the water. It's perfect. What do you think of the lemon?"

A summer shower had moved in, and my gaze drifted out the window toward the waterfront, taking in the weathered wooden causeway. Light from a nearby shop window reflected off the worn boards, now damp from the falling rain. Two people stood near the end of the dock, almost obscured by the awning of the gift shop next door. Wild arm movements led me to assume they were arguing.

I squinted to get a better view, but the steady rain made it hard to distinguish any details.

Beverlee tapped the table with the end of her spoon and pursed her lips. "Got better places to be today, dear?"

I shook my head. "No, that's not it at all. I'm just curious about what's going on over there." I pointed toward the pair in the distance, whose argument seemed to be getting more heated, based on the sharp arm gestures.

Beverlee peered over her shoulder, "Looks like somebody isn't happy."

"Do you know who it is?"

She picked her glasses up off the table and slid them on, then stepped over to the window. "I can't tell. Why?"

"No real reason, but it seems odd for somebody to be standing in the rain fighting." I didn't know how to explain to her that ever since I found Doris, I've been viewing everybody as a suspect. Sharing a bed with Old Bill's corpse the previous night hadn't helped.

Beverlee pulled her glasses off and dropped back into the chair. "I'm sure it's nothing." She gazed back out the window. "But you'll find out who it is in a minute. One of them is walking this way."

I busied myself with a plate of Swiss buttercream and pretended not to stare. As the figure approached, Beverlee let out a laugh. "Oh, it's just Dex." She smiled brightly as Kate's fiancé approached the café.

When he pushed the door open, Beverlee waved him over to our table. "Dex, come in out of the rain. I'm sure you remember my niece, Glory. She's here helping me pick out a couple of flavors for our wedding cake."

Dex looked me over slowly, his gaze traveling from my face down to my chest. I fought the urge to roll my eyes. It appeared good ol' Dex was still a boob man, so not much had changed there. He had aged a bit, his shaggy frat boy blond hair now short. He wore khaki pants and a sporty navy polo shirt, the hairs on his forearms damp from the drizzle. Time had been kind to him, unfortunately. It was always a shame when dirtbags didn't get what was coming to them.

He nodded and flashed a smile that seemed like it belonged in a toothpaste commercial. "Glory, yes, I remember. It has been a long time."

Not long enough, I thought, resting my hand over the open neck of my shirt.

Beverlee, as ever unaware of social undercurrent, said, "We were having our cake and noticed you out there in the rain. It seemed like you were having a serious discussion. Is everything okay?"

His gaze flicked to me, and for a moment I saw something like fear flash across his face. "Thank you for worrying about me, ladies, but all is well. I'm afraid it was nothing more interesting than a discussion about zoning laws." He chuckled. "You know how twitchy the county can be about their paperwork."

Beverlee nodded. "I do indeed." She gestured to the table. "We've got far more cake than we need. And you have your own cake tasting coming up, I believe. Can we offer you a sneak peek?"

His practiced smile oozed political charm. He leaned over and broke off a piece of chocolate hazelnut cake and popped it into his mouth. He leaned in and whispered. "I've always been a sucker for chocolate." Then he stood back up and nodded toward Beverlee. "Speaking of which, Kate made a fantastic batch of chocolate zucchini muffins for breakfast the other day. I hear I have you to thank for the recipe."

Beverlee gushed. "Well, yes. They're a favorite of mine this time of year. The zucchini is such a surprise. It keeps everything nice and moist. I'll be posting a follow-up pumpkin recipe on the blog next week. Tell Kate to keep an eye out for it."

"I will." He smiled, nodding toward me. "Good to see you again, Glory. Always glad to have another voter back in the fold. Now if you ladies will excuse me, I'm about to grab a cup of coffee to take back to the office." He held up the stack of papers he had in his hand. "A civil servant's work is never done."

Maple fondant got stuck in my throat as I held in an exasperated groan.

I focused on the papers he was holding. On the top was a real estate listing with a familiar picture at the bottom. The charming white cottage with the red front door was the same house we had broken into a few nights before. I waited until Dex turned away before I leaned toward Beverlee and whispered, "Was Doris thinking about selling her house?"

"I doubt it. She loved that place. She bragged about it all the time. They'd have to pry those keys from her cold, dead—"

My stomach turned, and I held out the palm of my hand. "Got it. Could you see what Dex was carrying? It looked an awful lot like a real estate listing for Doris's place."

Beverlee craned her neck to get a look at Dex, who was now in line chatting with another customer. "No. But hang on." She stood up and went over to the camera and leaned down to the viewfinder, making several adjustments. Then she came back over to the table, grabbed the remote, and shouted, "This is such fun! Let's take one last picture before we go get ready for the bachelorette party. Smile!"

I started to argue, but I saw the camera wasn't even aimed at us. It was pointed toward Dex, with the zoom lens at full extension.

"Here's to cake." I reached across the table to slide my

finger through the last of the vanilla bean frosting and popped it into my mouth.

⁓

AFTER WE LEFT THE BAKERY, we made a quick stop at the floral shop to review a few last details for Beverlee's bridal bouquet. The florist smiled as she unlocked the door. "I got the sword handle you ordered, and I was just cutting it down. Come in and let me know what you think."

We followed her into the shop, where she ushered us to a worktable covered in black ribbon in a variety of widths, red plastic flowers, and the grip of what looked like a toy sword that had been cut off at the blade, leaving just the hollowed-out handle.

"I will age it with bronze spray paint and some sandpaper, but it will work just fine as the base of your bouquet," she said, nodding to the other items arranged in front of her. "And I've gotten some fake flowers to play around with until the real ones arrive."

In keeping with the pirate theme, Beverlee had chosen roses so red they were almost black. With deft fingers, the florist wound them in tape and secured them to the handle, mixing in fluffy ostrich feathers and spires of twisted seagrass and baby eucalyptus. When she finished, she extended it toward us.

Beverlee's eyes were shimmering with tears. "It's almost perfect," she said, her voice a mixture of awe and delight.

"Almost?" I asked, looking at her in confusion.

She tugged open her endless tote bag and started digging around in the bottom, finally coming out with a white organza sack, which she emptied on the table in front of us.

A handful of beautiful antique brooches spilled out onto the surface, each an elegant piece of art in pewter and aged stone. "I wanted to include the people that aren't here with us today, so I'm planning to carry them with me down the aisle in my bouquet."

She picked up a small hummingbird encrusted in delicate pink and gold gemstones and held it out toward me. "This one's for your mama," she said. "To celebrate her free spirit."

I swallowed against the emotions rising in my throat.

"And this one's for my mama. She loved to garden; she would have loved to meet Matilda." She fumbled through the pile and showed me an iris with a central stone that looked like an old amethyst.

Her eyes were misty as she laid it down gently and pointed to an elegant butterfly sparkling with subtle swirls of brass and tiny diamond flecks. "This one represents Edwin's first wife, may she rest in peace."

Finally, she laid her finger on top of an intricately carved bumblebee and pushed it toward me. "And this one's for my first husband, Louis, the one who taught me how to love. He sure did know how to get stuck in my craw, but I still thought he was the bee's knees," she said with a saucy wink.

I remembered Louis. A big lumberjack of a man, he had passed away before I went to live with Beverlee. For years, she lit a candle next to the fireplace in his honor every evening, and she always blew it out with a kiss before bed. A lump lodged itself next to my voice box, and when I spoke, the sound was choppy. "That's beautiful, Beverlee."

The florist dabbed at her own cheek with the corner of her sleeve. "All weddings are special, but most brides want cookie-cutter bouquets full of orchids and carnations that will look good in pictures. They're lovely, but they lack the romance of a true, deep, complicated love story, one with a history."

Beverlee grinned and elbowed me. "See? I told you the sword was a good idea."

18

Just before eight o'clock that evening, I tugged at the hem of my far-too-short skirt and pushed open the door to Trolls. A crowd of women had already gathered on the roped-off waterfront deck, and they were well on their way to finishing a pitcher of strawberry daiquiris. Beach music hummed through the speakers and I bobbed my head to the beat as I took in the room.

Beverlee jumped up when she saw me come in. "This is my idea of the perfect day," she said as she motioned to nearby tables piled high with snacks. "We started with cake, and we get to finish with dessert."

White tablecloths and red and silver confetti covered the tables. One had trays of key lime tartlets, dark chocolate brownies, and pastel macarons. Next to it, another table was topped with bowls of chips and pretzels. "This is quite a setup. You did a good job covering the two major food groups: salty and sweet."

"Ian gets the credit for the food," Beverlee said, fluffing her hair. "He said the crab dip is a dry run for his sister's rehearsal dinner, so let him know if the recipe needs any tweaking."

Shirley stepped up to join us, stopping to give me a quick hug. "You've got to love a man who knows how to feed a woman. My favorite part of the day is when he comes into the Grind and Go for coffee." She fanned herself with her napkin. "Plain black coffee has never looked so sexy."

A woman I recognized as a teller from the Flat Falls Savings and Loan raised her glass. "I'll drink to that," she said over a mouthful of brownie.

"You'll drink to anything," Beverlee said, shaking her head. "Tonight, I would like to make a special toast to Bill Judson's daughter. I took a chocolate chess pie over to the funeral home this evening to pass along our sympathies, and she was kind enough to agree to let Edwin and me use her father's boat for our wedding. In fact, she thought it was a great way to honor him. True love always wins in the end."

Heather Judson, Old Bill's only child, had left town a few years before me and was rumored to have done time in the women's prison in Georgia for robbing a jewelry store when her no-good husband refused to buy her an engagement ring for Valentine's Day. Although I was normally a fan of an empowered woman, I drew the line at armed robbery in the name of jewelry.

I rubbed the back of my neck. "How much did you give her?"

"I didn't—"

"How much?" I asked, looking around for the first aid kit where Ian kept a bottle of pain reliever.

Beverlee gave a dismissive wave. "Okay, fine. Five hundred."

"You gave Old Bill's daughter five hundred dollars to let you get married on that creepy boat?" I shook my head. "Unbelievable."

"Never underestimate the power of a few Benjamins to help make your dreams come true, baby." Beverlee smiled and took a bite of mini cheesecake.

I sighed. "I'll be sure to stitch that on a pillow."

Beverlee took another sip of her drink and leaned in. "And speaking of dreams-come-true, have you spoken to Ian tonight?"

"No, I haven't even seen him," I said, although it wasn't for lack of trying. I looked over my shoulder toward the main bar.

"He won't come in here. I think he's afraid."

"Afraid of what?" I asked.

"A few members of the Methodist Ladies' Book Club got a little too handsy with him last week after their meeting took a rowdy turn."

I swallowed a laugh. There was nothing Ian would hate more than being at the center of the gossip circle's focus.

A shadow crossed my peripheral vision, and I felt his presence before I even saw him. He stood near the entrance to the room, his gaze locked on me. "Sorry to interrupt, ladies. I wanted to make sure you have everything you need."

A hoot came from across the room. A younger woman with long, dark hair and a tight red dress giggled and shouted, "I do, now that you're here."

"We've talked about this, Lucy. Don't forget I've seen your husband at the gym. I'm not about to take him on," he said, stacking empty glasses to carry them back to the bar. "Regardless of how beautiful you look tonight."

Lucy grinned, and catcalls and snorts of laughter echoed throughout the room.

Beverlee motioned me over to her side. "Glory, I'd like you to meet Lucy. She works for the Lifestyle section of the paper. If you ever need a decorating recommendation, Lucy's your girl. She's got an eye for design like nobody else."

"Welcome home, Glory," she said. A flash of uncertainty crossed her face, but then disappeared. "Beverlee talks about you all the time. It's like I know you already."

I remembered Beverlee mentioning Lucy in the past, too, but it wasn't flattering. She had called her needy and brazen. And if Beverlee, Queen of Overbearing, said that about you, it was probably best to steer clear.

I gave a small wave and added some distance between us. "It's nice to meet you."

"Can I ask you a question?" She stepped toward me, large tortoiseshell glasses bobbing up and down on a nose that was far too large for her pale, petite face.

I shrugged. "Sure, I guess."

She took another sip of her drink and leaned in. "When somebody dies, do their eyes stay open?"

I stepped back. "I'm not sure I—"

Lucy laughed, but her stare was intense. "I'm just wondering, you know, since you seem to have stumbled across not one, but two dead bodies in the last week. That's got to be some sort of record."

Beverlee stepped forward and put her hand on Lucy's arm. "Enough talk about bodies, girls. Lucy, why don't you go grab another plate? I whipped up a batch of sweet tea cookies this morning and I'd hate for them to run out before you get a nibble."

Lucy tilted her head, her eyes never leaving mine. It was like she was studying me.

I shifted uncomfortably and held up my empty glass. "No, I'll go. I need a refill anyway." I took a stuttering breath and turned toward the bar. "Excuse me."

Ian was easy to spot as I entered the main section of the restaurant. He stood with his back to me on the other side of the bar, wiping down one of the beer taps with a cloth.

Memories flooded through me again. Once upon a time,

he was my everything. But time and my big plans had ruined the easygoing smile he had once held aside for only me. And now, as I crossed the mostly empty restaurant, an unfamiliar tug pulled at my belly. I wanted that smile again.

I stepped up to the bar and tapped on the wood, hoping the noise would make him turn around. It wasn't likely he could hear it over the chaos from Beverlee's party, though.

Clearing my throat didn't make him turn, either. I was about to toss a peanut from the silver bucket on the bar at him when our gazes locked in the mirror above the sink. His eyes were dark and unreadable, his mouth turned down in a frown. He took his time wiping down the counter, then turned to face me.

He arched his brow as he placed the rag down on the counter in front of me. His voice was low as he leaned forward. "Did you need something?"

"I needed to get out of there," I said. My hand was still shaking. Lucy was right. I had seen two too many dead bodies since I'd been home. Even faced with the one guy who had been known to give me the good kind of tingles instead of the creepy ones, murder was a guaranteed buzzkill.

The corner of his mouth turned up slightly. "Not the party girl you used to be?" His voice was light, but he stared at me with focused intensity.

"You wouldn't believe me even if I told you."

"Try me."

I debated telling him the truth, the real reason I left Flat Falls. The reason I could never come back. But humiliation wound through me, and I looked away instead.

Ian stepped back, his eyes shuttered. "Can I get you a drink, then?"

"Sure. You're the bartender. Surprise me."

He chuckled. "I can do that."

He filled a glass with an amber liquid from the tap and slid it across the counter toward me.

I reached for it, ignoring the zing that shot through my skin when my fingers brushed his. I took a hesitant sip. Instead of the bitter taste of beer I was expecting, it tasted fruity and light. "This is good."

"I didn't figure you for a beer girl anymore. It's a local cider. Most of the women around here like it, and most of the men think it makes the ladies a little friendlier. It's a win-win for Team Bartender."

The bar was lit with a warm, amber glow. Music played through the speakers and, even though it wasn't crowded, people were enjoying heaping plates of food. "This looks like a fun place to work. How long have you been here?"

"Since the beginning. It's mine."

I jerked my head up in surprise. "You own it?"

He nodded. "There are worse things to do than live a dream."

I took a slow sip of my drink and avoided meeting his gaze. "I wouldn't know."

He leaned forward until his face was even with mine. "What happened to you, Glory?" he asked, his voice low and challenging. "What happened to the girl who was all salt and fire, the one who lit up every room like a damn Roman candle?"

I flinched and swallowed hard, fighting the familiar burn of shame swelling in my throat. "She grew up, Ian."

He pushed back from the bar and shook his head, his focus never leaving my face. "Too bad. I liked that girl."

Me, too. I fidgeted with the napkin underneath my glass. I could barely remember what it felt like to be her, to be care-free or self-assured. All I felt these days was lost and unbalanced.

He considered me for a moment, then finally spoke.

"After you left, the dream of this place saved me. Actually, Beverlee got me through."

I jerked my head up. Beverlee hadn't mentioned anything about Ian after I left town. "She did?"

He nodded once. "She took pity on me, brought me food, listened to me complain. She mothered me back into the world of the living again."

I smiled over the dull thud that settled in my stomach. Once upon a time, she had done the same thing for me. "That sounds like Beverlee."

"And when I had the idea for the bar, she was all in. She even talked Scoots into selling off a piece of property." He leaned against the counter behind him. "I wanted a place where people could come and hang out when life started to unravel."

"Home," I said, running my finger through the condensation on the bar.

He gestured at a group of patrons across the restaurant. "This is my favorite time of the year. Summer is ending, so it's mostly locals and their fish tales."

I smiled as I studied a group of men engrossed in a heated conversation about who caught the largest marlin that day. "I always thought it was sad when summer ended."

"The key is to enjoy it while it's here." Ian pointed out the back window where the edge of the bridge was still visible. "If you'll recall, we watched many summers come and go under this bridge."

"You mean you watched many cases of beer and pretty girls."

I was rewarded with the flash of his elusive dimple. "That, too."

He finished the last swig of his beer and rolled the bottle between his fingers. He nodded toward the man sitting at the other end of the bar with a stack of files and a double cheeseburger. "If I remember correctly, Gage became a real man for the first time about 15 feet from where you're standing. Molly Jean Bartlett in the back of an aluminum fishing boat."

Gage grinned and tipped the brim of the baseball cap he wore low over his eyes. "It was a good day."

Ian laughed. "Nothing says summer like a bucket of wine coolers and a game of spin the bottle with impressionable coeds."

He placed the empty beer bottle flat on the counter and twisted it back and forth.

"Nobody actually plays spin the bottle, Ian."

"Sure, they do. It's fate's way of playing matchmaker."

He let the bottle go, and I held my breath as it spun in a lazy circle, the mouth finally coming to rest facing me. A blush crept up my cheeks as our eyes met. "So, you're saying you let chance decide which girl was going to get lucky?"

"I'm saying I kept spinning the bottle until it landed on the cutest one."

I blinked once. Then again. Surely Ian Strickland, king of the admittedly well-deserved grudges, wasn't flirting with me. It was the spinning that made me dizzy, not the bartender. I was about to lunge for the voodoo beer bottle when Lucy clunked her empty glass on the bar next to me.

"The bride wanted me to ask if you have any Cher karaoke," she said as she glanced over her shoulder at the impromptu dance party underway in the other room. "And I think we might need some refills."

He pulled his gaze from mine and nodded at a server who was polishing glasses at the other end of the bar. "We'll take care of it."

After he delivered several pitchers of sangria to the party, Ian came back over to the bar. "Time to go."

He grabbed a key ring and a bottle of water, then ushered

me toward the door with a warm, firm hand on the small of my back.

I caught Beverlee's eye as we moved across the restaurant. She smiled and gave a little wave.

Ian whispered to a man standing in the doorway, handed him the keys, and pushed me out into the warm, humid air. "Let's get you home before you cause any trouble."

"I don't need you to walk me home, Ian. I'm perfectly capable of—"

"You don't have any idea what you're capable of," he said in a low voice.

We ambled down the boardwalk in silence and, except for me missing my step a time or two, it was uneventful. When we got to the steps leading up to the apartment, I turned toward Ian. "Thanks for the stroll, Prince Charming."

Ian laughed and shook his head. "Does that make you Cinderella?"

"Only if you kiss me." I regretted it as soon as the words left my mouth. I wasn't the kind of girl who asked for kisses. Not anymore.

Ian inhaled sharply and leaned his arm against the side of the building. "I'm not going down that road again, Glory. You damaged me enough the first time."

Heat burned my cheeks. "Ian, I'm—"

Ian held up a finger in response.

"What are you doing?" I asked.

Ian smiled, and I saw a flash of his dimple again. "Wait for it," he said.

I heard the tapping of dog nails on the metal stairs. Rusty skidded across the landing and came to a stop in front of us. A yellow ball bounced out of his mouth and landed with a *splat* next to my shoe, then left a slug trail of slobber as it rolled slowly toward my door.

Ian bent down and rubbed his hand through Rusty's

caramel fur. "I figured he'd be as much of a sucker for a damsel in distress as I am."

"How did he know we were here?"

"He must have heard us. He hangs out with Scoots during the day but tells her when he has somewhere to be."

I crouched to give Rusty a greeting. He flopped over on his back for a belly rub. I grinned. "You men are all alike, aren't you?"

Ian took my keys and opened the door. The apartment was dark, and as I reached in to turn on the light, Rusty scrambled to his feet. His low growl raised the hairs on my arms. "What is it, boy?"

Ian's strong arm snaked around me and yanked me behind him. "Stay here."

"Ian, what's—?" The words hung in my mouth as I got the first look inside the apartment. My head began to spin as I tried to make sense of what I was seeing. The coffee table had been pitched onto its side, its contents carelessly scattered across the floor. Splinters of wood from the toppled bookcase speared piles of clothes and linens from the bedroom. A kaleidoscope of dried pasta, crushed seashells, and glass shards littered the floor.

The whole place had been ransacked.

19

The police left the apartment after midnight, followed by Beverlee and Edwin, who had shown up within ten minutes of my call with a plate of chicken wings and a carafe of hot tea. They fussed over me until I begged them to go home.

Ian and Josie stayed even longer to help me pick up the mess.

"I'm sorry I didn't hear anything," Josie said. "Anderson Cooper puts me to sleep faster than a shot of tequila."

Nothing had been taken, so Hollis said it looked like a neighborhood robbery or somebody looking for drug money. "I'm going to increase patrols in the area to be on the safe side." He leaned in and lowered his voice to a whisper. "Will you be okay by yourself tonight?"

I didn't want to admit how unsteady I still felt, so I glanced at Rusty, who was curled up on the floor at my feet. "I have my own personal guard dog," I said with a hesitant smile. "We'll be fine."

His guard duty only lasted a short while, though. Within

a few minutes of everyone leaving, he had curled up against my leg on the sofa, snoring.

I tossed and turned most of the night, but found comfort in the warm, smelly body that spent the night guarding more than his fair share of the covers.

After the sun came up and the sounds of business as usual filled the streets around the apartment, I opened the door and motioned for Rusty to follow me. As much as I wanted to hide out in bed all day, I needed coffee. I also needed to clear up my embarrassing request from the night before.

Rusty followed me across the walkway to the seawall where Ian's boat was tied up. We had barely made it across before he flung himself onto the deck with a grunt.

After a fortifying breath, I stepped onto the boat behind him. I knew there was a proper way to ask for permission to board, but nobody had ever accused me of being proper. Least of all Ian.

Rusty let out a sharp bark just before the hatch scraped open, and I was staring at Ian's bare chest. All of a sudden, the large boat seemed tiny. "Morning, trouble," he said, his voice as rough as the stubble peppering his chin.

I shook my head. "No trouble here. I came by because I needed to return your dog."

"You could have just opened your front door," he said, tugging a worn-out T-shirt over his head. He studied me for a moment and his voice softened. "Are you doing okay this morning? I'm sure you were pretty shaken up after what happened last night."

I rubbed my hands up and down my arms as I thought back to the scare from the night before. "It turns out Rusty's pretty good company, although he's a champion bed hog."

Ian's eyes flashed briefly before he snapped his fingers.

Rusty, who had moved to a sunny spot on the boat's front deck, jumped to attention. Ian pointed to the pier. "Off."

Rusty scrambled to the edge of the boat. With a quick, high-pitched yap that sounded like the canine equivalent of "Aye aye, Captain," he deftly leaped to the dock.

"You're making him leave?"

"I'm heading out for a few hours," he said.

I pointed at Rusty. "He's not going with you?"

Ian shook his head. "No. He's not a good boat dog."

"What does that mean? He seemed like he was in heaven a second ago."

"Sure, here," Ian said and nodded out toward the open water. "Out there? Not so much."

"Is he afraid of the water?"

"Nope. Seasick."

I barked out a laugh, immediately covering my mouth when I caught Rusty's forlorn glance. "Your dog, the one who lives with you *on a boat*, gets seasick?"

"Laugh now, but it's not nearly as funny when you've got a hundred pounds of barfing mutt six hours offshore."

"Poor baby." I nodded with sympathy at Rusty, who had laid down on the dock with a solid *thunk*.

"How come he always gets sympathy? I'm the one who has to clean up after him." He smiled fondly at the dog, but when he looked back at me, the fondness disappeared. "Thanks for bringing him home."

I nodded but made no motion to leave the boat.

"Did you want something else?"

With a dramatic sigh, I leaned against the boat's railing as nervous tingles pulsed through my arms and legs. "World peace. I'd like world peace."

The corner of his mouth turned up slightly, and he continued winding a piece of rope around his muscled forearm. "Oh, is that all?"

I closed my eyes. "And nachos. The kind with cheese that oozes down your chin and lands on your shirt, but you can't stop eating because they're just too good."

He glanced down at the front of my shirt, then tossed the rope coil aside and shoved his hands into his pockets. "Nothing celebrates world peace better than a good plate of nachos."

I could see his facade cracking, and triumph bounced around like champagne bubbles in my stomach. I had almost gotten a smile. "Bras where the underwire doesn't impale you. A way to remember my bank account password since who has time for all those capitals and punctuation marks?"

He finally chuckled, and I wanted to fist-pump the air for making the coveted dimple appear, even if it was only a flash.

"Anything else?" he asked.

I placed my palm flat on the captain's chair in front of me, then said quietly, "I want to apologize for last night." I swallowed. "For throwing myself at you."

Ian leaned back and crossed his arms. The muscles of his forearms bunched up, reminding me yet again that Ian wasn't the lanky teenager I had once known. "I had forgotten all about it."

His response felt like the sting of a barb, quick and sharp. I moved toward the edge of the boat. "Oh, good." I gave him a dismissive wave. "I didn't want you to misunderstand... I mean, I wasn't thinking straight."

"Obviously," he said, a frown creasing his brow. "It's no big deal."

"Great," I said. "Wonderful. Well, I'll be going, then." My voice sounded foreign, high-pitched and squeaky.

I held onto the railing as I stepped out onto the dock. I was walking away when Ian called out from behind me. "Glory, wait."

I spun around, my pulse quickening. "Yes?"

Ian motioned for Rusty to follow me. "Like I said, I'll be gone for a few hours. You might as well hang onto your bodyguard."

RUSTY TAGGED along with me when I went to see Beverlee later that morning, and it turned out he was a popular escort through Flat Falls. Every time I stopped, he threw himself to the ground to stare up at passersby with expectant eyes, his pink tongue hanging out the side of his mouth. They stopped to pet him, and as he soaked up the attention, nobody glared at me, which I considered a win all around.

I usually found Beverlee in her garden at this time of day, but when I walked around to her side door, I noticed she wasn't outside. The chickens were wandering around the backyard, pecking at insects. Matilda watched me step up to the door and clucked in greeting. Rusty ran over to her, tail wagging. She ran under a nearby bush in response. Rusty whimpered, then sank to the ground in defeat.

I scratched him behind the ears. "Come on, buddy. No chicken dinner for you today."

I knocked on the door but didn't hear an answer. I looked toward the street to make sure Edwin's car wasn't there before I tried the door handle because I didn't want to barge in on them again. It turned easily, and I knocked with more force as I pushed my way into Beverlee's kitchen, Rusty panting at my heels.

"Hello?" I called. "Beverlee? Anybody home?"

A jolt of panic tightened my chest. Beverlee never left her door unlocked when she was gone. She didn't want anyone to come in and steal her secret recipes. And now with a murderer on the loose, there was a lot more at stake.

I walked farther into the kitchen, but a loud crash from behind the house startled me. Rusty barreled out the open kitchen door toward the commotion, barking loudly as he ran.

My feet slipped on the floor, and I hit my shoulder on the corner of the kitchen cabinet as I sprinted after him. "Rusty, come back!" I screamed, fear sitting heavy on my chest. I didn't want to lose Ian's dog... again.

I turned the corner into the yard just as Rusty wiggled his way under the bush where we had last seen Matilda. His low and menacing growl was followed by frantic chicken squawking. I couldn't get through the thick hedge of bushes, so I ran around the shed, hoping to grab Rusty before he had a tasty snack, but when I got there, I found him on the house side of the fence gate, the golden hair on his back standing on end and his eyes locked on a patch of chicken feathers resting on top of the grass.

"Oh no," I said, dread rising in my stomach. "Rusty, where's Matilda?"

He ignored me and continued to stare past the gate, a snarl stretched across his normally sweet face. He pawed at the ground where the chicken feathers were.

Behind me, a car door slammed, and as I made my way back around the shed I found Beverlee standing in her yard carrying a basket of fresh vegetables from the market.

"Glory, you startled me. What were you doing behind the house?" She leaned down to scratch Rusty's head.

I shifted back on my feet and avoided making eye contact. "It's Matilda," I said, looking over my shoulder toward the back fence. "There's been an accident."

Beverlee dropped the basket and rushed into the backyard, the dog close behind her. She stopped and looked around. "My girl? What happened to my girl?"

Rusty belched and dropped a feather from his mouth on

top of her shoe. I took a deep breath. "I think Rusty killed your favorite chicken."

AN HOUR LATER, I was sitting at Beverlee's table still trying to console her. Dark smears of mascara ringed her red eyes. Discarded tissues dotted the floor, and a cup of chamomile tea sat untouched in front of her.

"She was such a good girl," Beverlee sniffed. She finally stood and shuffled to the counter, where she picked up a yellow and aqua cookie jar adorned with a hand-painted image of a chicken. She held it out to me. "Cookie?"

I slowly stuck my hand into the cookie jar, unsure about etiquette rules for chicken mourning. "Um… thanks." I took a small bite of frosted sugar cookie.

"They were Matilda's favorite."

I wondered how a chicken had discovered she had a favorite cookie. "She had good taste." I raised the cookie in the air in salute. "To Matilda."

Beverlee dabbed a tissue under her eye. "To Matilda," she said as she popped another cookie in her mouth.

Our impromptu poultry wake was cut short by the kitchen door opening. Edwin rushed in and crouched next to Beverlee. "I came as soon as I heard."

"What a terrible day," she said in a watery voice and turned to bury her face in his chest. "Terrible."

Edwin pulled her in close, smoothing his hand down her back over and over until the tears stopped. "Matilda was a world-class chicken," he said and pulled away. He tipped her chin up with his finger. "Do they suspect fowl play?"

I snickered. "Nice one."

Edwin looked over with a wink. "Just trying to lighten the mood."

Beverlee swatted him, but the tears had stopped. She was chuckling when she stood to carry her dishes to the sink.

I turned to Edwin. *Thank you*, I mouthed.

Rusty whined near the door, so I got up to take him out. When I opened the door, Hollis stood there, a chicken tucked carefully under his arm like a football.

He nodded a greeting. "I got a disturbance call a few minutes ago from the Grind and Go. Customers couldn't get in or out because of an angry chicken pecking at the screen door. Wouldn't let anybody in or out unless they gave her food. Does this little lady belong to you?"

Beverlee ran toward Hollis, her arms outstretched. "Oh, Matilda, I thought I would never see you again."

She picked up the chicken and pulled her close, stroking her feathers gently.

Hollis cleared his throat. "Yes, well, try to keep her in your yard, will you?"

"She was in the yard," I said as I glanced down at Rusty, who was sitting at attention under Beverlee's feet, hoping to get another chance with his feathered friend. "We thought the dog had gotten her. She disappeared."

Hollis nodded toward the chicken. "Is she the only one missing?"

Beverlee nodded and continued to rub Matilda's back. "The rest of them are tucked away in the coop. Out of all my girls, she's the free-spirited one. Always exploring, getting into trouble, like my Glory. That's why she's my favorite."

She smiled for a moment, then her forehead wrinkled. "But if Rusty didn't get her, how did she get out? The fence in the back is tall enough that she couldn't have gotten over it even if she was highly motivated." She narrowed her eyes at the dog, who had the good sense to look down at the floor in shame.

Hollis nodded. "The gate probably came loose in the

wind over the last few days. Then when Rusty here made a move on her, she looked for an easy exit."

Beverlee shook her head. "I don't think so. I keep the gate locked back there behind the shed. You can't see it from the yard, so it always made me uncomfortable. I put a lock on it last year so I wouldn't have to worry about it anymore. It stays locked all the time."

"If you'd be willing to spare a cup of coffee, I'd be happy to go out and have a peek." Hollis hitched up his belt and nodded toward the coffeepot.

Edwin rolled his eyes.

Beverlee beamed. "Of course. And I'll even throw in some cookies."

Matilda clucked and Beverlee leaned down and whispered to the chicken, "Don't worry, I'll save you one."

Hollis returned a few minutes later, scowling. "I found where your chicken escaped," he said.

"You did?" I asked. "Where? She ran under the bushes. Then when Rusty ran after her, she disappeared."

Hollis picked up the coffee Beverlee had set out for him on the counter. He took a slow sip. "The gate in the back was wide open."

"But how—" Beverlee asked.

"The lock was cut clean off," he drawled. He reached into his pocket and pulled out a metal padlock with a broken hasp. "My guess is that Rusty here wasn't after the chicken, but after whoever was skulking around behind your shed." He calmly took another sip of coffee, then turned toward both of us and raised a brow. "Any ideas about who that might have been?"

20

B everlee's face paled, and she stumbled backward into the counter. "Somebody was in my yard?"

Edwin stepped forward and put a comforting arm around her, then guided her to a chair. "Sit, sit," he said, quietly stroking her hair. "Let's hear what Chief Goodnight has to say."

He faced Hollis, concern furrowing his brows. "How do we find out who did this? And who broke into Glory's house last night?"

Hollis stepped across the kitchen and looked out the back window. "First, we need to determine whether this was a robbery or something else. We've been having a lot of trouble in the warehouses near the waterfront. It could be that a new criminal element has taken up in the area and both of you were in the wrong place at the wrong time."

I raised a brow.

"The more likely situation is that the person who broke into your house, Beverlee, is the same one who robbed Glory last night." Hollis leaned over the back of my chair. "Glory, you said Beverlee's door was unlocked when you arrived?"

I nodded. "Yes, which was unusual. She always locks up when she's not here."

Beverlee agreed. "I didn't want anyone to come in here trying to steal my top secret—" She gasped and jumped from the chair. "My recipes!" She rushed down the hallway and threw open the door to my old bedroom.

A moment later, she returned with her laptop cradled against her chest. "They're safe," she said with relief, waving her free hand in front of her face like she was in the middle of a hot flash.

Hollis motioned to the computer. "You think somebody would break into your house to steal your recipe collection?"

"I know they would. People will give just about anything for a good roasted chicken recipe. I've had people begging me for mine for years."

She glanced over toward the door and told Matilda to cover her ears, then leaned toward me and whispered, "The secret is in the skin. You want it nice and crispy, so you have to make sure it's completely dry before you slide the bird in the oven."

"That's not a secret, Beverlee. I can't boil water and even I know that."

Her hands went to her hips. "Okay, Smarty-pants, how would you get the skin dry?"

I raised a brow. "Um… paper towels?"

She made a buzzer noise. "Only if you want to serve pedestrian chicken."

I grimaced at Edwin. "And nobody wants pedestrian chicken."

He hid his chuckle behind his fist.

Beverlee didn't even slow down. She crossed the kitchen and threw open a drawer, then pulled out a glossy black hair dryer. "This is how the magic happens," she said with a smirk.

"You blow-dry your chicken?"

Beverlee smiled and pointed to the awards stuck to the front of her refrigerator with magnets. "How do you think I won the blue ribbon at the county fair last year? By giving the judges exactly what they wanted."

"A fifty-dollar-bill and a complimentary tube of antacids?"

"Crispy skin," she exclaimed. "If you blow-dry the chicken skin before you put it in the oven, it stays nice and crispy."

I glanced at Hollis and Edwin. Their eyes were wide, and they were both nodding.

"Good tip," I said, wondering how the criminal investigation had morphed into a discussion about chicken grooming.

Hollis cleared his throat. "Can we get back to the matter at hand? We've had reports of suspicious activity down near the waterfront recently. It's possible some petty criminals broke in looking for drug money. It appears your prized recipe collection has been spared, but can you take a quick look around to see if there's anything else missing? Maybe Glory interrupted something before the intruder could get what he or she came for."

Beverlee clutched the laptop. She took a few unsteady steps out of the kitchen, returning a few minutes later shaking her head. "Nothing looks disturbed. My television and jewelry box are still there. I don't have anything else particularly valuable."

Edwin grabbed her hand. "You're the most valuable thing. I'm so thankful you weren't here when it happened."

I put my arm around her. "Me, too."

Beverlee squeezed both of us tight, then stepped over to the refrigerator. "All this talk of criminal behavior has made me hungry. Who wants some lunch?"

Her eyes were wide and glassy, and it was obvious she was transferring her anxiety to the one place she knew she could control. The kitchen.

"I could eat," Edwin said with a placating nod.

Hollis rubbed his stomach in agreement.

Beverlee stacked ingredients on the counter. She pulled out andouille sausage, shrimp, and cream, then started chopping a bunch of fresh herbs she had brought home from the market.

My stomach growled. Nobody ever went hungry at Beverlee's house, especially when she was feeling stressed. "What can I do to help?"

"I'm making smoky shrimp and a quick johnny cake." She pointed toward the pantry. "I've recently come into some cornbread mix. Can you grab a bag for me, baby?" she asked with a wink.

Only Beverlee could get away with cooking stolen food for the chief of police. I rifled through the contents of Beverlee's well-stocked pantry. I glanced over my shoulder. "I don't see it."

Beverlee pushed me to the side. "It's right near the..." She froze. "It's gone. Somebody stole my cornmeal."

21

After Hollis left and Edwin went back to work, Beverlee and I sat in her kitchen trying to figure out who had been sneaking around her home. "What would make somebody break into a house and steal cornmeal, Glory? It makes no sense."

I didn't remind her that she'd stolen the cornbread mix first. "Maybe it was a local kid, somebody who really likes fish," I suggested.

Beverlee shook her head. "You can buy seafood breading mix at every grocery store in the area. What's so special about that one?"

I thought about it. "Your hush puppies are one thing I missed when I moved away. I can't even smell fried seafood these days without getting misty-eyed."

She grabbed my hand and gave it a gentle squeeze. "Not everybody gets sentimental over fried dough, baby."

I smiled and sat up straight. "Did you ever open one of the bags?"

"No. I've been too busy for much cooking lately. Why do you ask?"

"I was wondering, what if the bags weren't filled with cornbread mix? What if they contained something else?"

She considered my suggestion for a moment. "Like what?"

"Drugs?"

Beverlee nodded, her brows furrowed. "I suppose it's possible. Hollis mentioned something about a problem they were having with the buildings down near the dock. I wonder if somebody is using those bags of mix to smuggle drugs."

My thoughts turned to the mysterious man I had seen on Old Bill's boat. "We need to track down Sunglasses Man. He's the key to figuring out this whole thing."

THAT AFTERNOON, I stopped by the Grind and Go for a half-dozen cranberry almond muffins, then wandered down the boardwalk to the police station. I had given Gage plenty of time to figure out Sunglasses Man's identity, but since he hadn't shown up on my porch with any information, I was resorting to bribery.

The station was quiet when I got there. The front desk was vacant, so I wandered back through the maze of sand-colored cubicles until I found him. He had his feet propped up on his desk, with a crime novel in his left hand and half a sandwich in his right.

"Busy day?" I asked dryly.

"I've been sitting at this desk since I got here this morning. I'm taking a break," he said, holding up the sandwich like a turkey trophy. "Want some?"

"I'll pass." I leaned my hip against the desk and offered the muffin bag. "But I brought you dessert. I thought you might be working overtime to catch the murderer and would like a treat."

He opened the bag and inhaled deeply, eyeing me with suspicion. "What do you want?"

I smiled, reaching out to rest my palm on his forearm. "I wanted to visit an old friend."

He shook his head and took another bite of his sandwich. "I'm not buying it. You're not the bring-somebody-muffins-out-of-the-blue type."

I sighed and sat down on the desk, then stole a potato chip from his plate. "Fine," I sighed. "I need information."

He leaned back in his chair and waited for me to continue.

"Remember that picture I sent you a few days ago?"

He nodded slowly.

"I need to know who he is."

He sat forward and frowned at me. "I can't comment on an ongoing investigation, Glory."

"Come on. I'm not asking you to give me his entire criminal history. I just want to find out who he is."

His voice took on a serious tone. "And what will you do if I tell you?"

I jumped to my feet. "Aha! You do know who he is."

He crossed his arms in front of his chest. "Yes, I do. But I won't share that information with a civilian."

I grabbed the bag of muffins. "Then I'll be on my way."

He looked down at the bag. *Gotcha*, I thought.

"Listen, Glory," he said. "We're dealing with a real bad guy here. He's not your run-of-the-mill criminal. He's got ties to some nasty industries—drugs, money laundering, smuggling, you name it. You wouldn't believe some of the things the Maritime Crimes office sent over."

I nodded, pointing to his computer screen, which

showed a grainy image of the back side of a boat docked at the Flat Falls Marina. "Is that his boat?"

Gage groaned and clicked the image closed. "No." He shook his head hard. "I can't have you running off to confront him by yourself."

"Got it," I said as I dangled the muffins in front of him. "So, what's his name?"

∼

GAGE WOULDN'T GIVE me his name, so I only left him one muffin. I took the rest over to Josie's apartment. I gave her the rundown on what I had seen during my visit to the police station and handed her my laptop.

Within minutes, she had pulled up the town's webcam and zeroed in on a marina located less than two blocks from the pawnshop. She pulled up the same feed Gage had been watching.

The camera was focused on a large boat that rocked gently against the current at the end of the dock. But this boat wasn't anything like Beverlee's fixer-upper pirate ship. Where Old Bill's boat sported worn teak and shrimp nets, this one was shiny white vinyl and polished chrome. Old Bill's boat was built for a seafaring man. This one had been custom-made for a drug lord who liked fast cars and half-naked women slippery with suntan lotion and gold-digger dreams.

A few clicks later and the screen displayed the boat's registration information. "His name is Anton Burke," she said.

I looked at her in surprise. "Impressive. What's his story?" I asked.

She scrunched her face and held up a finger as she continued to type with the other hand. "Looks like he runs some sort of import business." She turned her head to the side and swiveled the laptop around toward me, a clear image of Anton's face occupying the screen. "Not bad looking, though. He has nice hair."

I felt a shudder roll through me. "Nice hair does not make up for the fact that he probably keeps women's heads in his freezer."

She acknowledged that with a shrug, then pointed at the laptop screen. "Here's an article from a few years ago from a jewelry trade show. It looks like your guy knows his gems."

"He's not my guy." I squinted to get a better look at the picture. It showed Anton Burke in an expensive-looking black suit with his arm draped across the bony shoulders of an attractive redhead wearing a silver sequined column dress. A large emerald necklace rested in the hollow of her throat.

Anton wasn't looking at the camera. Instead, he had his eye on the redhead's neck. "Looks like they caught him ogling the merchandise," Josie said.

"Or he might be trying to peek down her dress." I leaned back against the seat and took a deep breath. "What if Anton's import company isn't what it seems? What if he's the piece that ties all this together?"

Josie nodded slowly, then turned her attention back to the computer. "Maybe. But even if he's into some illegal business activities, that doesn't mean he's a murderer."

"Wait," I said, as I caught a quick flash of movement on the screen. "Can you zoom in?"

"No, it's a fixed-length camera. What is it?"

I squinted and leaned forward. "I thought I saw something."

We both stared at the screen. I was afraid to blink, so I held my eyes open until they watered. I didn't want to miss anything.

After a few minutes without action, I leaned back and stretched my neck. "I could have sworn I saw—"

"There," Josie said, pointing to a spot on the screen. "You were right. There's somebody in the cabin."

We watched as a beam of light sliced across the dark cabin window. "Anton wouldn't be using a flashlight on his own boat."

It was getting dark, and the picture from the camera had gotten even more grainy, so we both continued to watch, eyes squinted, our heads tilting back and forth as we tried to make out the details of what was happening on the boat.

Finally, I stood up. "It's too hard to make anything out from here. I'm going to get a closer look."

"Bad idea, Nancy Drew," Josie warned. "This isn't a game you're playing. There's a killer out there, and my guess is he's better at this than you are."

"This might be my only chance to figure out who killed the wedding planner," I said, zipping up my jacket before moving toward the door. "And if there's a chance we can prove Beverlee's innocence before her wedding, I have to take it."

Josie stared at me for a long moment before giving a single jerk of her head. "Fine," she said. "But take your phone. I'll keep watch from here and call you if I see anything unusual."

I headed through the alley behind the pawnshop and toward the marina. The wind had picked up and was whipping sails and flags against their metal masts like a bell choir performance.

Anton's boat was docked at the far end of the marina. I didn't have the advantage of being at the top of a pole like the town's webcam, so I stepped out onto the dock, wincing when my foot hit a squeaky board. I crouched behind a deck box and waited for a murderer to come running down the platform toward me.

There was no movement on any of the boats in response to the noise, though, so I wondered if Josie and I had imagined seeing someone in the cabin.

I had just decided to walk down the dock toward Anton's boat when I heard a thud on the wood behind me. I turned to find Rusty, tail wagging, galloping toward me.

I glanced around to see if anyone had spotted him, but he was marauding unnoticed. I patted his head, and he gave my hand a slobbery kiss. "Hey, boy. I'm glad to see you, but you've got to go."

I pointed toward the grassy area on the other side of the sidewalk, but Rusty didn't budge. He just kept looking at me, his tail thumping against the dock's wooden planks in rhythm with the water below.

"Go home," I said, nudging him with my knee.

Nothing.

"Fine." I sighed. "But stay out of the way."

I had just turned toward the last boat slip, Rusty happily glued to my leg, when my phone vibrated in my pocket.

"Get down," Josie said after I connected the call. "He's heading your way."

I was midway down the dock with limited options for camouflage. I slipped behind a kayak mounted on wooden rafters on the side of the landing next to Anton's boat, and tucked my fingers through Rusty's collar, pulling him close to my side.

I held my breath for several seconds. Finally, the cabin door opened, and someone slowly stepped out. The shape of the body looked like a man, but he wasn't tall and broad enough to be Anton Burke.

He made his way around the side of the boat, stopping to open the gear box and shine down into the bottom with his flashlight. He slammed the box closed with a curse that echoed across the water, then deftly leaped over the side of the boat and onto the dock less than ten feet away from me and Rusty. A lump formed in my throat as familiar blond hair shined in the moonlight. What was Dex Harvey doing on Anton's boat?

I was hopeful Josie could help me get off the dock unseen, but as soon as I held the phone to my ear, her panicked voice signaled that something else was wrong.

"Glory, get out of there," she warned. "Now. I think Sunglasses Man is heading in your direction."

I looked to my right. Dex Harvey was still standing at the stern of Anton's yacht.

And on my left, Anton Burke was heading for the marina.

With nowhere left for me to run, I tugged on Rusty's collar, plugged my nose, and stepped backward into the inky water.

AN HOUR LATER, after I had paddled my way to the other side of the marina with a wet, chubby dog in tow and climbed over a seawall slick with decaying chum left by the day's fishermen, I stepped onto the porch I shared with Josie. She was already there, her hair wild and the phone in her hand.

"You disappeared," she shrieked. "Why didn't you call me back?"

I reached into my pocket and pulled out my dripping wet phone and held it out to her. "Mine's broken. Can I borrow yours?"

She handed it to me, and I dialed Beverlee's number.

After half a dozen rings, she answered with a dramatic

sigh. She and Edwin were in the middle of a candlelight pre-wedding couple's massage.

"Why did you answer the phone, then?" I asked, trying not to sound frustrated.

"I'm still waiting to hear back from the musician to see if he can play the *Wedding March* on his hornpipe. When I didn't recognize the number. I thought this might be him."

I scrubbed my hand down my face and squeezed my eyelids closed. Only Beverlee.

She moaned and my eyes popped open. "Did you need something, baby?" she asked.

I filled her in on Anton and what I had seen at the marina. "It was Dex, Beverlee. Kate's fiancé."

She paused. "That's odd. What is Dex doing with that shady fellow?"

Edwin's muffled voice echoed through the phone and Beverlee said, "Eddie reminded me we took a picture of Dex at the bakery. I'll send it over. Can you and Josie look at it tonight? We'll reconvene in the morning." She giggled. "But not too early."

A few seconds later, Josie's e-mail dinged to signal the receipt of Beverlee's message. I nodded to Josie. "Open it."

She clicked open the picture, enlarging it to display on the screen. Beverlee's new digital camera had put out a high-resolution image. Dex was a blur in the foreground, but the bakery case behind him was crystal clear.

I sighed, wondering what I'd have to do to get another cup of that hazelnut frosting.

Josie laughed. "So, you struck out. He's a politician, right?"

I nodded.

"Then it should be easy to figure out his schedule of public appearances."

I wrinkled my brow. "I doubt he'll spill his secrets in the

middle of the town square, Jo."

"That's not what we need." After a few more keystrokes, she whooped and spun the computer toward me. "There's a ribbon cutting for the new town hall building tomorrow morning."

I nodded, not understanding why she'd be so excited about a municipal building. "Okay. Sounds exciting."

"It absolutely is. The old one smelled like foot cheese."

"Then I'm glad they're getting a new one," I said, rolling my shoulders and stealing a glance at the clock."

"You don't get it, do you?" Josie asked, her brow raised.

"Obviously not."

She pointed at the screen with an unladylike snort. "Who goes to ribbon cutting ceremonies?"

Realization dawned slowly. "Politicians."

Josie slammed her hand on the table. "Bingo. And if our wannabe senator will be at the ceremony, there's one place he won't be."

"His office," I said with a smile.

DEX HARVEY'S real estate development office was in an upscale professional building near the waterfront. Each building faced the water, and the back was tucked into a small series of alleyways. Sand-colored stone covered the building, and each pair of offices shared a green scalloped awning and a glass-enclosed vestibule.

"Park in front of the dentist's office," Beverlee instructed as we pulled up. "I can always say I had a denture emergency if anybody questions us."

I tilted my head. "You don't even wear dentures, Beverlee."

"But I could," she said. "And nobody would ever ask for

proof."

Good point. I started to climb out.

Beverlee grabbed my wrist and held me steady. "We need to wait for Scoots to get here."

"Why is Scoots coming?"

Beverlee rolled her eyes. "How else are we supposed to get into the building?"

"Is she a locksmith and an attorney?" I asked.

Beverlee raised her hand in a wave as Scoots trudged up the sidewalk. "Don't be silly," she said. "She owns this building."

Of course she did.

We joined Scoots at the door as she shuffled through the two dozen or so keys jangling around a large metal ring. "It's here somewhere," she said.

I turned and pretended to be admiring the planter nearby. Beverlee crossed her arms and raised her brows at Scoots. "If you don't hurry up, I really am going to need dentures."

"Hold your horses, woman," she said, then held up a key in triumph. "I found it."

Scoots turned the key, and we tumbled into Dex's suite. "Back here," she said, and we followed her past a small reception area and a glass-walled conference room. "His office is in the rear corner."

When we walked into the office, Beverlee clicked on a desk lamp. "We've got about ten minutes. Let's see if we can figure out what pies Mr. Politician has his fingers in."

Beverlee took the filing cabinet next to the back window. She pulled open the top drawer and rifled through files, reading the labels aloud. "The causeway improvement project. Doc Hennessey's office. And, huh, did you know Shirley was looking at renovating the restaurant?"

Scoots opened the closet door and peered under Dex's

mahogany leather rolling office chair. She shrugged when I gave her the side-eye. "You never know where people hide things."

His desk was neat but well-used. A black metal file sorter in the corner contained color-coded folders for his current projects. "There's nothing interesting here," I said.

I inspected his glossy white drafting table, sitting at an angle in the corner. I ran my hand over the sleek, cool surface.

Scoots came up behind me. "These tables are cool," she said, and lifted the drawing surface with a smile. "They always have such nice storage nooks."

Beverlee rushed over. "Did you find something?"

I lifted a legal-sized folder and flipped it open. "More plans," I said.

Beverlee snatched it out of my fingers and shuffled through the pages. "That's the whole waterfront area. He's got pictures of all the buildings down there, along with blueprints."

I shrugged. "So what? He's a developer. Looks like things any developer would keep around."

She pulled out a grainy photo and turned it around. "But why does he have a picture of your Sunglasses Man right in the middle of it?"

A loud boom of male laughter sounded from the front of the building. We scrambled to return the folder to its hidden compartment. Beverlee dove across the desk and clicked off the lamp.

"We can't go out the front," Scoots whispered.

I looked around the room frantically. "There." I pointed. A small window led from Dex's office to the back alley.

We rushed over and flipped the lock on the window sash. I gave it a firm shove, and it moved up about an inch.

Scoots turned and raised a brow. "You've got to be

kidding if you think I could even fit my pinky through there. I like cheese too much."

I pushed again, and the window shifted open with a loud *creak*.

"Be quiet," Beverlee urged, shushing us with a wave of her hand.

"Out." I pointed. "I'll give you a boost."

I locked my fingers together and held them down for her to step into. Scoots was the first up, and she climbed out the window and landed on the ground with a soft thud.

I pointed at Beverlee and motioned that it was her turn. She stepped into the cradle of my hands, and she shimmied out the open window.

"Grab my arms," I whispered. I heard the voices drifting back toward the office. "And hurry."

I stretched toward the sky and stifled a shriek when I was pulled out the window in one quick movement. I tugged the window back down and spun around. "You guys are much stronger than I gave you credit—"

The words stuck in my throat as my gaze traveled from a well-worn pair of jeans to broad, muscled shoulders and whiskey-brown eyes staring at me in amusement. "Hello, Glory."

"Ian," I said with a curt nod.

Scoots wasn't successful at convincing Ian we were climbing out the window as part of a routine building safety inspection. "It's my building, Ian. Are you saying I don't have a right to inspect it the way I think is appropriate?"

"No, ma'am," he drawled. "I'd never accuse the three of you of being inappropriate."

He narrowed his eyes toward me, and I gave a jaunty wave. "We're heading over to change the air filters at the pawnshop now, Ian. As you know, safety is important. Care to join us?"

He declined and turned a frown toward me. "You just can't stay out of trouble, can you?

Beverlee punched him in the arm. "Used to be that you liked a little trouble, Ian. What's got you so grumpy this morning?"

He released a deep sigh. "I'm tired. Stayed up a little too late last night thinking about mermaids."

I coughed and turned to go. Ian grabbed my wrist and leaned in until his mouth was inches away from my ear. "Want to tell me what you were doing slinking around the dock last night?"

"I'm not sure what you're talking about," I said, motioning toward Beverlee, who had walked just far enough away to pretend she wasn't eavesdropping. "I spent last night having dinner with the bride and groom."

"Interesting. I could have sworn it was you I saw shimmying up the seawall in the dark when I was on my way home from work." He picked up the end of my hair, letting it slide through his fingers. "I saw long, dark hair."

"Nope, not me." I hurried my steps and finally made it to the car. I clicked the unlock button, then opened the door and slid into the driver's seat, motioning for Beverlee to hurry up and get in.

"Black from head to toe. Curves for days," he continued as he put his forearm over the top of my car door, preventing me from closing it. "Curves I would never mistake for somebody else."

My pulse quickened, but I shook my head. "Sorry."

He stepped back, a faint smile across his lips. "My mistake, then. Must have been a dream."

I waved, then gave the door a tug to pull it closed.

Ian tapped on the window. I rolled it down halfway and raised my eyes to meet his. "Yes?"

"Next time dry my dog off before you send him home."

22

When Beverlee's wedding day finally arrived, I was waiting outside the café when Shirley flipped the open sign. The lock clicked, and I pushed through the door. I dropped my purse on the counter and pointed toward the menu. "I need coffee. The biggest one you have. And a blueberry muffin." Then after a moment, I added, "No, make that two. And some bacon. It's going to be a long day."

She smiled and began assembling my order. "I understand today's the big day."

I nodded. "Yes. Cobbling together a wedding at the last minute during a murder investigation has been quite a challenge."

The bells over the door jingled to signal another customer's arrival. Shirley leaned over and whispered, "I heard the chief and Gage talking yesterday, and it sounds like they're getting close to figuring out who did it."

"I hope so. It will be nice to have this behind us."

"It sure will. I can't imagine starting off my married life with that hanging over my head. But Beverlee's not your normal bride."

I thought of the day I had ahead of me. "You've got that right. I get to spend my morning wrangling inflatable parrots and arranging twinkle lights on the mast of a disintegrating pirate ship."

She laughed. "I can't imagine what their honeymoon will be like."

"Hopefully calmer than their wedding. Edwin said the stress of planning the wedding has gotten to them both, so they're heading to the Bahamas to hang out, eat seafood, and drink fruity things with umbrellas in them."

"Sounds nice," she said.

"Doesn't it? I could use a tropical vacation myself," I said as I broke off a bite of muffin.

I SPENT the rest of the morning running around Flat Falls dealing with one crisis after another until I could finally focus on my job as Beverlee's matron of honor. Apparently, that included running around her backyard with a gilded bird cage trying to capture a chicken intent on keeping her freedom.

"Oh, come on, Matilda. It's just for a few hours." I waved the cage in front of her and made kissing noises. No luck. She continued clucking and running. I let her go for a few minutes, wondering if she would tire herself out like a toddler.

I leaned down and tried to flip open the door to the cage, but it was stuck. Grabbing a stock from the ground, I tried to pry it open, but the wood was too thick. I needed something the size of a coin to slide into the latch and loosen the rust that had sealed it shut.

I fumbled through my purse, but I couldn't find any coins. The only thing roughly the same size was my old engagement ring, which was loose in the bottom of my wallet. I pulled it out and turned it over in my hand, surprised to not feel the familiar tug of sadness.

Might as well put it to use. I slid the gold band into the side of the latch and twisted. With each turn of my hand, the fastener loosened, and after the door finally popped open, I pumped a fist in the air.

When I looked down at my hand, I noticed that the twisting motion of the ring had popped the main stone loose from one of its prongs. I tapped it with my fingernail and the fake diamond fell out into my palm.

I dropped the setting back into my bag. Maybe Scoots would help me get some money for the gold. I wasn't ready to throw the stone away, though.

I was trying to figure out where I could keep it without losing it when Matilda trotted by. "Come back, chicken. We've got a wedding to get to."

She didn't come back.

I tucked the fake diamond into my bra and crouched down. I motioned for Matilda to hop into the cage. She clucked and paraded the other way.

None of the other chickens were in the yard. I nodded up toward the coop and tried the guilt angle. "Your friends aren't acting crazy. They're probably in there being well-behaved because they know what a special day this is for Beverlee." I sighed. "You don't want to ruin her big day, do you?"

Matilda trotted over to the edge of the flower bed and hopped on top of the stones lining the bed. She stopped moving and stared at me.

"So, we're going to do it the hard way, are we?" I put the cage on the ground and faced off against her. I pushed up my sleeves and took a deep breath. "Fine. Let's do this."

I had just started taking tiny steps toward the chicken when the gate screeched open behind me. I looked over my shoulder to see Ian, arms folded across his chest, struggling to hide a grin. Rusty stood beside him, wagging his tail.

Ian pointed at Matilda. "You heard the lady. Get in the cage."

Matilda didn't move.

Ian reached into his pocket and pulled out a cookie. He broke off a piece and held it out to her. "Please," he said softly. Matilda responded by running toward him, her head bobbing and an eager clucking springing from her chest. As soon as she got close enough, Ian fed her the cookie, bent down, and scooped her up. Instead of immediately depositing her in the cage, though, he pulled her into the crook of his arm and gently stroked the feathers at the back of her head.

The hussy ate it up.

I walked over to them. "You carry cookies in your pocket?" Not a bad idea. A man who carried around junk food for emergencies was pretty hot.

He smiled, and I couldn't keep from watching his mouth. That dimple was addictive. He held out the rest of the cookie. "Want some?"

A flush crept up my cheeks, and I shook my head. "How did you know we were here?"

"I was delivering food for the reception and Beverlee mentioned Matilda might need some help."

I stared at him in disbelief. "You came to rescue the chicken?"

"What can I say? I'm a sucker for a chick in distress." He continued to stroke the silky feathers on the chicken's back. "And Rusty wanted to pay his girlfriend here a visit."

At the sound of his name, Rusty's tail started wagging so hard I wondered how he could still stand up.

Ian nodded his head toward the open cage. "Is this Miss Matilda's party bus?"

I smiled. "Yes, but I've got to get her dressed first."

His eyes widened. "You're playing dress-up with a chicken? This should be interesting."

I stuck my hand into my pocket and pulled out a piece of stretch lace trim. I held it out to Ian. "Beverlee gave me orders to tie it in a bow around her neck so she'll look pretty for the ceremony." I reached out toward Matilda's neck. "Hold still."

Matilda didn't hold still. Instead, every time I leaned toward her, she clucked loudly and pecked at my finger. "Ow. Stop that." I pulled my hand back and gently massaged it.

Ian chuckled, then pulled the lace from my grip. He wrapped it, one-handed, around Matilda's neck. She didn't peck at him. Instead, she sat perfectly still and soaked up his attention.

When I grabbed the ends of the lace from Ian's hand to tie the bow, she pecked again.

Ian tried to hide his smile. He pushed Matilda farther into the crook of his arm so both of his hands were free, then he took the lace back and tied it in a bow. "There. All done," he said, tucking her safely in the cage.

I glared at Matilda and massaged my temples. "Cluck you, too."

The dimple flashed in Ian's cheek. "Come on, ladies. Let's not fight. You both look beautiful." He turned toward me, his eyes narrowing. "Especially you."

I fought the urge to pat my hair. "I'm not even dressed for the wedding, Ian."

"Doesn't matter," he whispered, then stepped back and shook his head. "You've always been tough to resist."

I couldn't help but laugh as I pointed to the dirt on my arms and the chicken feather stuck to my leg. "That's me. Irresistible," I said, moving my pointer finger up to rest on the center of his chest. "And you've been doing a pretty good job of resisting me since I came back. We're not even friends anymore."

"Aren't we?"

"No. We're exes, not friends."

"I didn't realize they were mutually exclusive," he said, a smirk playing at the corners of his lips. "Seems a shame to let a history like ours go to waste."

My voice got quiet, and I dared to meet his stare. "That's what I'm talking about, though. The history between us. You can't have forgotten how it ended." I tried to step around him, but everywhere I stepped, Ian was there. He was a hard wall of man and memories and the one mountain I didn't have the energy to climb today.

"Well, it *is* hard to forget a girl who grinds your heart into the gravel like a used-up match."

I swallowed hard, unable to get rid of the boulder-sized lump sitting in the back of my throat.

He held his palm out. "Listen, I get that you had to leave. I get that you wanted bigger and better than podunk Flat Falls and the lovesick kid that came with it."

"Ian, that's not—"

His face was strained, and thin ropes of muscle flexed in his jaw. "But you were it for me. You and your big dreams and smart mouth." His eyes lowered to my mouth, and desire flashed across his face.

I wasn't sure how to reply, so I stood there shifting from side to side.

"You were a beautiful bride, you know. Exactly how I imagined."

I jerked my head back and looked at him in surprise. "How did you…?"

"Beverlee," he replied.

"She showed you the pictures?"

Ian shook his head. "No, she told me what was happening before the wedding. I think she imagined me charging in on my valiant steed to sweep you off your feet."

I took a deep breath, trying to slow the hammering of my heart against the walls of my chest. "You were there? Why didn't you—"

"Because you didn't want me. I saw you walking down the aisle and thought about running after you. But you chose that douchebag in the skinny pants."

I thought back to my wedding day and the custom-fitted tuxedo Cobb had worn. It wasn't Clint Eastwood-level manly, instead skewing more toward modern metrosexual. I rolled my eyes. "It wasn't his best look."

He shoved his hands in his pockets. "I might be old-fashioned, but I'm a firm believer that the only person who should see a guy's jewels on his wedding day is the bride."

I chuckled, still surprised by Ian's confession.

"So, yes, I remember everything." He took a step forward, and suddenly he was in my space. The air shifted, and the hot flutter of panic as confusion and desire slid through my veins. He moved closer until his face was inches from mine. "Do you remember, Glory?"

I turned my head, afraid for him to see the truth. In a whisper, I replied. "Yes."

His warm fingers sent waves of heat through my chin as he guided my gaze to meet his. "Good."

Then he dropped his hand and walked away, leaving both me and Beverlee's lovestruck chicken staring after him.

23

"Are you sure a rum bar is a smart idea?" I asked Beverlee as I finished chalking in The Barrrrr is Open on a tabletop sign. I thought of all the potential hazards of having an open bar on the back of a moving ship and grimaced.

She laughed, then handed me a roll of red tulle and a stack of pre-printed recipe cards. "These are the signature cocktails. Make sure you tell the bartender to push the Dark and Moody. It's my recipe, made with rum, root beer, and pomegranate seeds. Delicious and very sexy." She winked and turned to walk away. "Now I've got to get ready. My dress just arrived, and I'm dying to see it."

I started wrapping tulle around the nearby chair backs. "Beverlee, wait," I called.

She turned and looked at me, her brow wrinkling with concern. "What is it, baby?"

Her crisp linen blouse was cool under my fingers as I pulled her into a hug. "Thank you for trusting me with your special day. You'll be a beautiful bride." And despite the gold brocade tablecloths and the black Jolly Roger flag that I had hoisted over the wedding arbor at the boat's bow, I realized how much I meant it.

"I'm glad you're here," she said and took a step back, cupping my face in her palm. "Have you ever thought about coming back to Flat Falls for good?"

"Not really." I lied.

"You should," she said, tucking my hair behind my ear before letting her hand fall to her side. "You'll always be welcome here."

"Funny. You might be the only one who thinks so." I shifted back and forth on the balls of my feet under her gaze.

Beverlee grabbed my hand and squeezed. "Don't let somebody else tell you how to live your life, Glory."

I swallowed over the lump in my throat. "Everybody in town believes we had something to do with Doris's murder. It hasn't given people the warm fuzzies. Just yesterday I was at the grocery store and somebody I didn't even recognize asked me about that time I backed into the fire hydrant during the Christmas parade. The mayor's office had to close for a week because of the flooding. People are still bitter."

Beverlee waved her hand in the air. "You can't park. Big deal. Other people don't get to decide who you are, baby. Only you get to do that."

"Nice words from somebody in the throes of wedded bliss," I said with a grin. "But just because you're full of bliss, it doesn't mean the rest of us get to be happy, too."

She rested her hand on top of mine and leaned in close. "You don't always get to choose happiness, baby. Sometimes things will stink to high heaven, and sometimes you'll get your heart broken."

I nodded and gazed out over the water so I didn't have to make eye contact.

"But you do have a choice about whether you let unhappiness pitch a tent in your heart like a vagrant mule."

I snickered and turned toward her. She had a faint smile on her face and was regarding me with gentle kindness.

"You can't go back," she said softly. "No matter how much you want to, you can't change the choices you made or the bad things that happened. All you can do is pick up the best pieces from the pile of what's left behind choose to not let them define you."

"She has a point, Glory."

We turned to see Hollis leaning against the boat's cabin, arms folded across his chest. "Flat Falls would be downright boring without the Wells women," he said with a smile.

"Hollis," I said. "What are you doing here?"

He stepped forward and addressed Beverlee. "I came to give you a wedding gift. We made an arrest in the murders of Doris Sadler and Bill Judson this morning," he said, shoving his hands into his pockets. "You are no longer an official suspect. You can leave the country for your honeymoon."

"What?" I asked. "Who?"

"We received information that a longtime resident was involved in illegal activities targeting Flat Falls business owners, particularly those along the waterfront district. We've got her on money laundering, fraud, and two counts of murder," he said. "And to think, she did it right under her own boss's nose."

I whipped around. "Wait, you're saying…"

His face was grim. "Yes, early this morning, we took Magnolia Winters into custody."

I WAS ALMOST giddy when I pulled open the door to the Flat Falls Police headquarters. It wasn't every day you got to visit your childhood nemesis in the slammer.

I signed in at the front desk and said hello to Gage, who

was filling a ceramic cup from a coffee pot near the main desk. "I hear it's a great day to nab a murderer."

He took a slow sip from the cup and narrowed his eyes. "You're a little too chipper today."

"I'm just glad you figured out who did it. It was disconcerting to have a killer on the loose."

He tilted his head and stared at me for a moment before speaking. "How well do you know her?"

"Who, Maggie? I've known her since we were kids, same as you. Why do you ask?"

He ran his free hand through his hair, leaving the ends sticking up. His clothes were wrinkled, and dark shadows ringed his eyes. "I was just thinking about how we never really know people."

I nodded, lowering my voice to match his. "Are we talking about the same girl who pulled the Homecoming crown right off Ruby Fowler's head in front of God and everybody because she didn't want to get second place?"

Maggie had also stolen that poor girl's diary from her locker and photocopied the most embarrassing pages, then tacked them up all over school. High school was humiliating enough without somebody outing your crush on the principal or the fact that you bleached your arm hair to avoid looking like a Saint Bernard.

"That was something," Gage said, wistfully. "I haven't seen a catfight like that in years."

"Maggie is a vain, conniving woman who wouldn't hesitate to slit the throat of anyone that got in her way."

He nodded. "They're coming up here later to take her to Raleigh for processing. They'll make sure the case against her is rock solid."

"About that," I said. "I need to see her before she goes."

Gage shook his head. "No can do, Glory. We've got a

strict protocol around here. Letting strangers in to see a suspect is not in the rule book."

I laughed and pushed my way past him. "Don't be silly, Gage. You and I both know she's the first murderer you've had around here in ages, so there aren't any rules to follow. You're just winging it. And besides, I'm not a stranger. I'm an old friend wanting to check on her during this horrible ordeal." I batted my eyelids at him for effect.

"Sorry. I wish I could." The corner of his mouth lifted in a half-smile and I could tell he was trying not to laugh. "But not even that impressive show of feminine wiles will get you in there."

"Oh, come on," I said. "I need to find the seating chart for the wedding this afternoon. Beverlee had a question about the number of chairs that are coming, and her contact isn't answering his phone. She's worried everybody will need to stand. I need to get the vendor packet from Maggie. Simple, in and out."

"Glory, I told you—"

I pulled out my phone and scrolled through my contact list. "Okay, but you need to explain that to Beverlee. She always had a soft spot for you. Maybe she won't kill you because you ruined her wedding." I let out a tragic sigh. "Although I don't know what she will do with all those lobster hand pies. She brings them in fresh."

He held up a palm to keep me from continuing. "Lobster hand pies?"

I licked my lips. "The mushroom cream sauce is practically orgasmic."

His cheeks were pink as he leaned forward and peered down the hall. "Can you ask her to save me one?"

I stood on tiptoe and kissed his cheek. "I'll bring you a whole plate."

He nodded and stepped aside. As I passed him, he whispered, "Down the hall, last room on the right. There should be an officer outside. Tell him I said it was okay for you to talk to her for a minute." His eyes narrowed. "But only a minute."

I gave him a jaunty wave over my shoulder. "Thanks, Gage. I owe you one."

As I made my way down the hall, I noticed there wasn't a guard outside the room like Gage had indicated. Through the window in the door, I could see Maggie hunched in a chair, her arms crossed in front of her. It looked like she was asleep, but her face was red and puffy.

I rapped on the door two times with my knuckle and turned the knob. Maggie's eyes flew open, and she scrambled to sit up in the chair.

"Well, hey, Magnolia. Fancy running into you here." I walked over and sat down in the chair next to her, kicking my feet up onto the coffee table with a thump.

She scrubbed her hand down her face and turned toward me. "Are you here to gloat?"

"Why would I do that? It's obvious you've had a hard enough day." I paused for effect, then leaned in. "Bless your heart."

"Why are you here? I have nothing to say to you."

"I thought I'd check on you before they haul you off."

"What do you mean?" She flashed a panicked glance toward the door. "Who?"

"You didn't know?" I felt a twinge of regret for gloating, but then I remembered the time she offered my training bra to the boys' junior varsity football team for a game of capture the flag, and my remorse quickly vanished.

Her eyes got big, and her chin quivered. She stared at me for almost a minute before speaking again. "There's not much time. You're my only hope."

"I'm not Obi-Wan Kenobi, Maggie. I don't think I have any hope to offer you."

She leaned forward in her chair. "I didn't do it, Glory. Despite how much you hate me, surely you know I'm not a murderer."

I raised a brow. "They don't arrest people for fun, Maggie." At least I hoped not.

She focused on her cuticles. "It's no secret that Doris and I had our troubles. But it wasn't because of the business." She raised her head and lowered her voice. "It was because she was blackmailing me. Remember that night I found you and Beverlee in her house? I was looking for the proof she had."

I leaned back in my chair and eyed her with practiced caution. "What did she have on you?"

"I… I'd rather not say."

I stood up to leave.

"Glory, wait. I'd rather not say because if it gets out it could ruin somebody's life. Somebody I care about." She paused. "And somebody you care about."

The desperation in her voice made me turn.

"I need to find it," she said. "But I've searched everywhere, and I still came up empty-handed."

The door opened, and Gage stepped in. "Social time is up, ladies." He motioned for Maggie to stand, then guided her toward the door. "Your ride will be here in five minutes."

I wiggled my fingers in the air. "Enjoy your trip."

Maggie's terrified glance stopped me from going any farther. Her tan skin had taken on an almost green tint, and her eyes were glistening with unshed tears. And despite, or maybe even because of, our shared history, I was overcome with the need to comfort her.

"It's going to be okay," I said quietly.

She nodded once and straightened her spine before turning back toward the door. Gage put his hand on her back to lead her out the door, but Maggie stopped with one hand on the door frame and looked over her shoulder. Her eyes were pleading, and the words tumbled out quickly. "They've got to be in her office. There is a safe in there. I only saw it once when I came back after I had forgotten something one night. It's behind the Monet print on the wall."

"I don't know what the combination is, but her birthday was on the first of October." She stared down at the floor. "Promise me you'll check. The pictures must be in there."

"Pictures?" I was suddenly intrigued.

Maggie's shoulders slumped. "Yes. Doris had pictures of me and the man I love."

This was getting interesting. I stepped toward the door. "And you want me to find them so you can prove your innocence?"

She shook her head, her fingers turning white where they gripped the door. "No. I want you to find them so you can destroy them."

24

The sun was setting by the time I got myself cinched into the gown's black silk corset and stopped by Beverlee's to pick up Matilda and her bedazzled cage. Before we headed to the marina for the ceremony, I wanted to make one final stop.

I reflected on my conversation with Maggie at the jail. It would be so easy to let her take the fall, but what if she was innocent? Guilt pressed its heavy fingers into my chest as I pulled the car to a stop in front of Weddings by the Sea.

I leaned over to grab a flashlight out of the glove box and climbed out of the car. The pirate dress was dangerously low cut, and I had to adjust it before heading over to the building's entrance.

As soon as I stepped away, a loud squawk came from behind me. I walked back over and flung open the door. "Matilda, would you be quiet?" I grumbled. "It's hard enough being inconspicuous with twenty yards of red lace attached to my hips. I don't need you letting everyone know I'm here."

I grabbed a beach towel, then threw it over the cage. I

closed the door and smoothed my skirt. Matilda let out another disgruntled screech before I even made it five steps from the car.

"Hush," I said, stomping back over to the car. "What's with the yelling?"

After shooting her a glare to show her I wasn't up for chicken games, I dug through my purse on the back seat until I found a cookie. I might not be in the mood for games, but I'm never above bribery.

I held it up to the side of the cage and made clucking noises, thankful that Beverlee had sent me that YouTube video on how to speak Chickenese.

"I have a cookie." Cluck. "It's a sugar cookie, your favorite." Cluck cluck.

Matilda glanced at me, then at the cookie. She didn't eat it. Instead, she pulled her head back and bellowed.

I tossed the cookie back into the car and glanced around to make sure we had avoided unwanted attention. Because the tourist season had ended, the boardwalk was empty. Considering I was dressed like a pirate hooker and was hauling around a tantrum-throwing chicken, I considered that a good thing.

"Fine," I said. "But you're not getting the cookie."

My fingers curled around the carved loop on the top of the cage. With a grunt, I dragged it out of the car and lugged it across the parking lot. I lifted a flowerpot to find the key Maggie had mentioned. I checked over my shoulder to make sure nobody was around, then let myself into the building.

The place was as spotless as it had been the first time I visited, and as I walked past the coffee table, I nudged the stack of bridal magazines with my knee so they were no longer perfectly aligned. I nodded once and kept moving.

The door to Doris's office wasn't quite closed, so I pushed it open with Matilda's cage and approached the desk. I set the chicken down on the floor and flicked on the flashlight, slowly scanning it until it landed on the Monet print on the far wall. I slid my hand along the frame but couldn't find any hidden buttons that made a safe appear.

It was a big piece of art, so I pushed aside a potted plant on the credenza and climbed up to get more leverage. I stretched my arms around both sides of the print and lifted it from the wall. A large safe dominated the space behind the painting.

I reached into my pocket to pull out the slip of paper where I had written Doris's birth date, Maggie's best guess at the passcode. I entered the numbers with shaking hands.

The safe beeped three times, and the lock turned red.

I tried again, my stomach flipping with increasing anxiety as I pressed each number.

Three beeps. Red lock.

Doris was the kind of woman who made notes about everything. Surely, she kept a list of passwords handy. I looked around the office.

I climbed down from the credenza and turned toward the desk. I flung open drawers and rifled through the contents. Nothing.

I ran my hand along the underside of the desk just in case a secret agent button would appear to open the safe. No such luck.

Putting my hand to the front of my dress to keep it from popping open, I squatted down and peered under the chair. Matilda took that moment to screech. I jumped in a panic, heart pounding and arms flailing. I knocked into the credenza, causing the plant to teeter, then crash to the ground.

I scrambled to grab the tumbleweeds of fake moss and straw to get it put back together. A tiny triangle of white peeked out from under the vase on the floor. With shaking hands, I unfolded the paper and almost whooped when I saw a series of numbers written in neat blocks. "Good job, Doris," I said. "I knew you were too organized to not have it here somewhere."

I turned to the safe and carefully entered the code. When I hit the final digit, the light on the front of the safe turned green and I heard a loud click. "Yes!" I pumped my fist in the air. I turned the dial and pulled open the door.

The large safe was almost empty. At the top of a small stack of folders was a manila envelope with the name Magnolia written in flowery cursive on the front. I pulled the envelope out, inspecting the front and back for a clue of what was inside. When I couldn't find one, I slid a finger under the flap until I felt the pop of separating paper. "Oops," I whispered.

I pulled out a thin stack of photos. I shined my flashlight on the top picture. Yep, that was Maggie, all right. A lot of Maggie.

It looked like someone had taken the pictures through a window with a long lens. Maggie undressing. Maggie reclined on the bed. Maggie entangled in the very naked arms of Dex Harvey.

"No," I whispered. "Maggie was getting it on with the soon-to-be senator? No wonder she didn't want these pictures to get out. Talk about a scandal."

Kate would be devastated when she found out about her fiancé. And Ian wouldn't be happy about this, either.

At the bottom of the stack of pictures was a written offer for the sale of Doris's cottage, signed by Dex. My heart thudded against the wall of my chest as I remembered seeing him on Anton's boat. He was the connection to Sunglasses Man, the one who tied everything together.

I inhaled sharply, the room spinning around me.

Dex killed her. Dex killed her, and Maggie was willing to take the blame.

I had to get to the police station before they hauled off the wrong person. Despite what Maggie wanted, I couldn't let her ruin her life over a man, especially one as slimy as Dex Harvey.

I put the pictures back into the envelope and laid it on the desk. I turned back toward the safe to close it. As the flashlight swept across the back, the beam passed across a small painting standing flat against the rear wall. Only the open back of the canvas was visible. I slid it out with shaking fingers.

I turned the painting toward me, not surprised to find that it was the same kind of racy painting Doris had stashed all over her house. It appeared Maggie wasn't the only one with a secret lover.

This one was a faceless man, much like the others. Painted in mostly grays and blues, it showed the front view of a muscled torso lightly peppered with chest hair. I ran my finger along the smooth lines of the man's chest, stopping when I reached a dark tattoo. My eyes widened as I moved the light to get a closer look. A dark anchor stretched across the naked man's broad chest, its crown flanked by sharp and deadly prongs.

I stepped back, my mind swirling with confusion. I had seen that anchor before.

Suddenly, the light flicked on. I turned toward the door to see Edwin standing there, arms folded across his chest. He was wearing a loose-fitting white shirt, tucked into black pants. He had a red sash tied across his chest and a shiny cutlass tucked into a scabbard at his waist.

"Edwin," I gasped and put my hand across my chest to settle my racing heart. "I'm glad you're here. We've got to go to the police station. Maggie didn't kill Doris."

He stepped forward and grabbed the painting, then chuckled. When he did, the front of his shirt gaped open, revealing the same faded tattoo as the man on the canvas. "You're a good kid, Glory. Why did you have to ruin everything?"

I stepped backward until my back was against the credenza. I pointed at the painting. "She knew you," I whispered. "Before Beverlee. Doris knew you."

I examined the picture. It was painted by a woman who was intimately familiar with her subject. Knew his moods, his emotions, and every inch of his body. My head jerked back to Edwin. "She was in love with you."

The pieces started falling into place. It wasn't Dex or Maggie or Anton that killed Doris. It was Edwin.

He stepped toward me, and I saw a flash of the pistol he had tucked into his waistband. "Sometimes women make bad choices." He shrugged.

My heart sank, and a sharp bolt of terror wrenched me backward. Edwin, the man Beverlee had welcomed into her home and her heart, was a killer. A cold-blooded, lying murderer.

Panic shot down my spine with a sharp zap and I reached back to the credenza to steady myself.

I suddenly remembered Edwin's story about his former wife. He hadn't seemed that broken up about it. "Doris was your wife," I said.

"Enough," he said, grabbing my arm with an unrelenting grip. I stumbled forward, tripping and landing with a hard thud on the ground. The room was spinning like the terror that was churning around in my head. Edwin bent down, his cold voice missing the Southern lilt it had carried just that morning. "It will break Beverlee's heart when you miss the wedding. I'll pass along your regards, though. I'll tell her you couldn't take the painful memories of your own failed marriage and that you ran away… again."

My vision blurred as I fought to blink away the sting of building tears. "She won't believe you," I whispered.

"No?" He fixed me with his cold gaze. "I imagine she'll believe me over the kid who left her alone all these years."

I recoiled, feeling the harsh stab of guilt. I pushed to stand up and turned to face him, my hands fisted at my sides with false bravado. "There's no way I'm letting you marry my aunt today."

He chuckled, then motioned to a man standing on the other side of the door. Anton slipped out of the shadows, a coil of rope dangling from his hand. Edwin spoke to him. "Get rid of her. Hide the body somewhere she won't be found for a while. Then come join us for the reception. I can't wait to introduce you to my bride."

Edwin reached into his pocket and pulled out a burgundy velvet bag just like the one I had seen in Doris's drawer. He tossed it to Anton. "And get these ready for my honeymoon."

Edwin tucked the pistol back into his pants and straightened his sash, then he picked up Matilda and walked out the door.

AS ANTON STEPPED TOWARD ME, I desperately searched for some way to fight him off. The room was mostly bare since the police had taken the computer and most of the files as part of the investigation.

He jerked his chin toward the door. "Let's go, cupcake," he said gruffly.

I pointed at the velvet bag he had clenched in his fist. "What's in the bag?"

"You don't get to ask the questions today."

"Doris had a bag just like that, but it was filled with rocks."

He raised a brow and stepped toward me, his glare menacing.

I put my hand up and stepped backward. "They're not just rocks, are they?"

He tucked the bag in his pocket. "You don't get it, do you?" He took two more steps toward me, blocking my escape route. "I don't mind killing you right here if that's your preference."

I calculated my odds of making it past him to the door. I was never a runner, and my hips were too round to be considered lithe. There was an exceptionally low chance I could slip by. But I had nothing to lose, so I bent at the waist and charged toward the door.

I almost made it, but he threw an arm out as I barreled by, his meaty hand digging into my shoulder. One sharp tug and I stumbled back into the room, landing on my behind in the middle of the floor.

He hadn't even shifted from his original position. Escape would be more difficult than I thought.

Anton reached into the back of his pants and pulled out a gun. He motioned toward the door. "On your feet. Now."

"That's what I was trying to do," I huffed. I slowly climbed to my feet and walked sideways around the exterior of the room. I didn't want to turn my back on him. I tried to delay by making small talk. "Where are we going?"

He put his hand on my back and shoved. "Move."

We made it to the front door, and I peered outside hopefully. Surely somebody nearby would be able to help me. I took a deep breath, ready to scream as soon as the door opened.

Anton saw through my plan. He leaned in and got close

to my ear. "Don't even think about it," he whispered and held up a finger. "First thing I'll do is shoot you in the head." He put up a second finger. "Then I'll go find your aunt and do the same to her. It would be a shame to have to blow somebody's brains out on their wedding day. All that blood doesn't mix well with bridal white."

I shut my mouth, and he pushed the door open. Despite my hopes, nobody was milling around on the boardwalk. Nobody jogging or walking a dog. Nobody.

I was alone.

Anton threw open the back of a food service van and shoved me inside. I had just enough time to pull the ruffles of my pirate skirt inside before he slammed it closed.

There were no windows in the back of the van, so although I tried to remember the turns he took, I couldn't. I was a rag doll, bouncing from side to side against the metal interior as he drove. When the van finally came to a stop, disorientation sloshed through my conscience. The crunch of his boots on the gravel outside the door sounded like a monster slowly chewing bones.

He threw open the door and pulled me out into a familiar clearing. We were at Old Bill's fishing shack. "What are we doing here?" I asked.

He ignored my question and pulled me to the dock next to the shack, where a mid-sized sport fishing boat had been tethered to the small pier. It wasn't a boat for tooling around the canals or making social calls. No, it was made for going deep. Ocean deep.

As we approached the dock, I gave a sideways glance toward the water, wondering if I should make a jump for it right there.

Anton nodded toward the water. "Go ahead. I hear it's like shooting fish in a barrel." He motioned to the inlet, his voice dropping low. "I wonder if the sharks make it this far inland if they smell a buffet."

I stood there a moment, estimating the chances that he would be able to hit me if I jumped in the water. Before I could move toward the water, he scooped me up and threw me over his shoulder. He walked down the dock and deposited me over the side of the boat in a tangle of leather and lace.

I felt the boat dip under his weight as he climbed aboard.

He stepped past me, removing the lines from the side of the boat. He fished the keys out of his pocket and started the engine.

As we started to pull away from the dock, something caught my eye from the shore. A blur of golden fur streaked across the lawn and leaped out over the water, landing with a resounding *thud* next to me. Rusty trotted over and sat down, his tail thumping on the deck of the boat. He looked from Anton to me expectantly.

"What is that dog doing here?" Anton asked over his shoulder. "I should make him swim back to shore."

I knew Rusty was able to swim, but it was getting dark and we were gliding further and further away from the dock. I didn't want to risk something happening to him because of me. "No," I said. "Just take him back when you're… through with me. Don't hurt him."

Anton's brow furrowed, and he rocked back on his heels. "What kind of monster do you think I am, lady? I wouldn't hurt an innocent dog."

My jaw dropped open. "But you'll hurt an innocent woman?"

He nodded once, pressed the throttle, and the boat sped off toward the open water.

25

The boat pulled out farther into the water, and the comforting sight of land soon disappeared. I wound my fingers through Rusty's fur and held on as we bounced over the waves.

I thought about diving overboard, but it would have been easy for Anton to reach out and grab me. I've never been a speedy swimmer. And as he reminded me, there are sharks in this water.

As we sped along toward our certain death, Rusty seemed to be enjoying his joyride. His pink tongue stuck out the side of his mouth, and his ears flapped in the wind.

I looked around the boat for something to use as a weapon. A fishing pole, a spear, a grenade. Anything. But no such luck. The only thing I could see was a fisherman's net scrunched up in the corner near the engine.

Anton focused on the horizon, and the boat propelled across the water at high speed. Now and then, he'd check over his shoulder to make sure I was still where he put me. He put his hand on his gun and gave me a sharp glare. He was frightening enough without adding in the extra menace, so I didn't move a muscle.

I glanced down at Rusty, who was panting and swaying back and forth with the rocking of the boat. Great. "Now's not the time," I whispered into his fur. "Don't get sick on me."

He leaned his head against my leg, sighed, and whimpered once.

I searched for a way to distract both of us from our impending doom. "Look." I pointed at the fishing net, a yellowing tangle of old rope and blue Styrofoam floats. "Balls."

With that, his ears perked up and his eyes searched the deck until they landed on the net. He swayed for a moment longer, then sprinted across the boat, feet skidding and tail wagging, until he bounced off the far side. He grabbed one of the floats and pulled. But when it didn't come loose from the mass of net, he dropped it and glanced back at me like I had been playing a trick on him.

I tried again. I motioned with my chin. "Rusty, ball."

His tail thumped once on the deck as he gazed back and forth between me and the net. He liked tug-of-war almost as much as playing fetch, so he overcame his queasiness and attacked the ball with gusto. He pulled and tugged until he freed the section of rope, then happily trotted toward me, dragging the net taut across the boat.

Anton turned. When he saw what Rusty was doing, he kicked at him with his shoe. "Make him stop," he shouted.

I pretended like I couldn't hear him over the wind. I cupped my hand around my ear. "What?"

He said it again.

I shook my head. "Still can't hear you," I shouted.

He threw back the throttle and turned quickly. The boat slowed, then came to a jolting stop. He pivoted and started toward Rusty, gun in hand, but the dog was whipping his new toy back and forth in a frenzy.

When he saw Anton turn to glance at him, Rusty assumed he wanted to play, so he eagerly ran toward him, a torpedo of boundless doggy energy. One hundred pounds of canine momentum slammed into him, and without time to brace for impact, Anton was knocked backward into the side of the boat. The gun fell from his hand and skittered across the deck, and the velvet bag tumbled from his pocket as he struggled to regain his footing.

As Anton stumbled toward me, his ankle got tangled in the net. He looked down to untangle it, and I reared back and ran toward him with my full force, arms pushed out in front of me.

I caught him off guard and, with one large shove, he flipped backward over the side of the boat, one leg still wound through the fishing net still clamped in Rusty's mouth.

Anton fought to grab hold of the boat, but his fingers slipped.

I grabbed the net, flinging it overboard as fast as I could. The end was attached to a hook on the side of the boat. The float was still held securely in Rusty's mouth. I tugged the net. He wouldn't let it go.

"Rusty," I said. "Release."

Nothing.

"Let go."

He cocked his head, but still held the net firmly between his very large teeth.

I pointed to the other side of the boat. "Cookie!"

He dropped the ball and turned.

Rusty bounced across the boat in search of a treat, and I pushed the throttle, quickly putting distance between Anton and me. He was still trying to untangle himself from the net and screaming threats in my direction. He bobbed up and down in the water, his head disappearing beneath the surface and then popping back up, his mouth spewing curses and seawater the whole time.

I leaned down and retrieved the velvet bag that had fallen out of Anton's pocket. I shook the contents into my hand. Not rocks, after all. Diamonds.

Edwin and Anton weren't smuggling drugs in those food packages. They were smuggling diamonds. Quite a few of them, from the looks of it.

Although I thought about letting Anton tread water in the open ocean for a while, I didn't want to let him die in shark-infested waters, so I reached back and grabbed the life preserver from its position under the rear seat. I threw it overboard and gave him a jaunty wave. "You're going to want to hold on," I said, then hit the throttle again.

The net was still wrapped around his leg, but he had wound his arms through the life preserver and was bobbing up and down in the boat's wake. As the line tightened, it pulled him partway off the surface like a water-skier, his frenzied display of head motions and spewed curses lost to the sounds of the engine and splash of the waves.

The wind pulled and twisted my hair, and the sea spray crusted it against my face. I grabbed the radio to call for help, but the handheld receiver came loose in my hand.

I looked down at Rusty. "What do you say about stopping a wedding?" I shouted over the wind.

Rusty responded by throwing up on my shoe.

I STUDIED the compass on the control panel and turned the boat back to shore. I used to skip school with a girl whose

father had a boat like this one. I never imagined that one day I would flee from a murderer in one exactly like it.

I pushed the boat as hard as it could go while keeping Anton afloat, and it only took a few minutes for us to catch sight of land. I kept going until the familiar dock came into view.

Rusty's body was pressed into my side and I feared he might reintroduce the contents of his stomach... again. I gave him one last scratch behind the ear and slowed the engine.

Old Bill's decrepit boat loomed before me. White twinkle lights wound up the mast, bright red tulle floated from the railings, and the crowd of wedding guests spilled over from the deck to the dock nearby.

The speedboat came in fast toward the dock, hitting the wooden structure with a jarring *thud* and bouncing off the dock's rubber bumpers. Beverlee was right. I was terrible at parking.

As the boat ricocheted away from the dock, I looked across the water and saw Beverlee and Edwin, hands joined, under the arbor at the front of the Old Bill's boat.

The boat continued to float away from the dock, and as Edwin leaned forward to kiss Beverlee's cheek, I realized I didn't have time to mess around with trying to dock the boat properly.

"No!" I screamed. I hiked up the layers of my pirate skirt and jumped into the water. I came to the surface and sputtered, my legs and arms tangled in its endless yards of blood-red lace.

I couldn't figure out how to unwind myself from the fabric's swirling fingers, so I unfastened it out of frustration. I kicked out of the skirt and watched it float away like a harlot jellyfish.

I had just righted myself when I heard a loud kerplunk

behind me. I turned my head to see Rusty paddling toward me.

I kicked my way over to the dock, but there wasn't a ladder. The tide was low, so the dock was at least two feet from the top of the water. I was wondering how I'd pull myself out of the water when a strong hand reached down and grabbed my forearm and yanked me up onto the dock.

Ian.

He leaned in until his face was almost pressed to my ear. His voice was low and warm. "Looks like you lost your skirt."

"Hold that thought," I said, turning to run barefooted across the warm wooden planks of the dock toward the boat. As I approached, I saw Hollis standing a few feet behind the crowd, his arms crossed tightly, his mouth flattened into a grim line.

When he spotted me, his jaw dropped. "Glory, where are your pants? What is…?"

I seized him by the hand and yanked him behind me, elbowing my way through the partygoers lined up along the water's edge. "No time to explain. I need you to help me stop the wedding."

He pulled his arm free and stopped. "It's too late," he said. "She's marrying him."

"Not if I can help it." I leaped over the back railing of the boat, my damp feet skidding on the weathered wooden surface.

I made it up to the bow just as Edwin grabbed Beverlee's hand and brought it to his mouth.

I put up my fists and turned to face Edwin. "Get your hands off her." Although I tried to sound menacing, like vintage Clint Eastwood, my voice was high-pitched and panicked, and I more likely sounded like a Smurf. Either way, I was not leaving that boat until I broke up their wedding.

Beverlee gasped and turned to face me, her eyes filled with unshed tears. "Glory," she said. "I thought you left."

I jerked my head toward Edwin. "He lied."

Beverlee looked back and forth between us. "I don't understand."

"Your fiancé is a con man," I said. "And a murderer."

"What are you talking about?" she asked, confused. "And where are the rest of your clothes?"

With a frustrated grunt, Edwin released the deck lines, and Old Bill's boat floated away from the dock. The guests already onboard watched Edwin and me in alarm.

He marched toward us holding the hilt of his metal cutlass. He grabbed Beverlee by the elbow and yanked her quickly toward him, securing his arm firmly around her chest. The sword's blade was resting against the underside of her chin.

"Edwin, it's not the time for jokes." She laughed and tried to squirm out of his grip.

"Quiet." His voice had lost any sense of softness, instead turning brittle and harsh. As he backed up slowly toward the edge of the boat, he narrowed his gaze and spoke directly to Beverlee. "I'm getting off here," he sneered, spittle forming at the corners of his mouth. "Darling."

I tried to think of something to distract him and I remembered the fake diamond I had shoved into my bra earlier that afternoon. Realizing I might as well put something from my failed marriage to good use, I reached in and pulled it out, then raised it to the light. "I've got your diamonds, Edwin."

He jerked his head toward me and lowered his voice. "Those are mine. How did you get them?"

"Your friend Anton gave them to me before he took a swim in the ocean. Let her go and I'll give them to you."

"I had it all planned," he said, his eyes locked on the

stone. "And you had to come back and mess it up. You don't belong here."

The blow hit its mark with startling accuracy, and I felt the sharp sting of tears as I slowly stepped over to the edge of the boat, holding the stone over the water in my open palm. "You're probably right. But this is your last chance."

He didn't move.

I turned my hand over and watched as the symbol of my own happily ever after disappeared into the murky water below. I gave Edwin a smug smile and tucked my hand back into the cleavage of my dress. "Shall I continue?"

He pressed the blade even harder into Beverlee's skin. A single drop of blood slid down her neck. "You know I'll do it, Glory. Go big or go home, right?"

"Edwin, stop. It's over. We know the truth." I turned toward Beverlee. "Remember that poor, dead wife you memorialized in your bouquet? She was also your wedding planner. And it turns out that her death was a lot more recent than Edwin led on because he killed her. They were involved in a scam to use your name and new product line to smuggle diamonds to the Bahamas."

Beverlee squirmed and glanced up at Edwin. "Eddie, what is she talking about?"

He pulled her in tightly and continued to back up. "Did you really think we were soul mates? Did you really buy into all that happily ever after business?"

The color left Beverlee's face, and she put a hand across her chest. "Well, yes, I…"

Edwin's cruel laugh echoed across the water. "Naive old woman."

She squinted off in the distance and tilted her head like she was trying to figure out exactly what he had said. After a moment, she took a resigned breath and her head fell forward.

I stepped toward them, prepared to catch her if she collapsed. Instead, she reared back, her head crashing into Edwin's chin with a distinct *smack*. The cutlass clattered onto the deck.

"Who are you calling old?" she shouted.

Blood spurted from Edwin's nose and spread across his white shirt. He cursed and clamped his fingers across this face to stop the flow. Beverlee twisted free and stumbled across the boat toward me.

"That's right, you geriatric geezer," came a shout from the stern of the boat. We all turned to see Scoots step out from behind the cabin. In her hand was an antique pistol. She pointed it at Edwin. "Now dance."

She took the gun and motioned toward the back of the boat. "There are a couple of officers of the law right behind me who would like to have a stern word with you, Mr. Calhoun. If you'll step that way."

Edwin looked back and forth between the three of us. "You're crazy. All of you are crazy."

Scoots bobbed her head. "Probably. Now get going."

The hum of a small outboard motor had us turning to see Hollis and Gage approaching the boat in a police vessel.

Hollis boarded first. He raced over to Beverlee first and looked her up and down. "You okay?" he asked gently.

She bit her lip and nodded.

He turned toward Edwin and zip-tied his hands behind his back. "What I don't understand is why you would go and mess it up with a woman like this."

I smiled. One of these days, he would tell her the truth about his feelings.

Hollis motioned toward Scoots. "Where did you get the gun, Scoots?"

"This old thing?" She shrugged and pointed to the cabin. "It was attached to the wall in there." She turned it toward her face and peered down the barrel. "I think it's a decoration."

"You can put the weapon down now and leave it to the professionals." Hollis extended his hand toward her.

She stiffened and turned, finally dropping the pistol in his outstretched palm. "Are you calling me an amateur?"

Hollis laughed. "Never."

Beverlee stared at Edwin for a moment before raising her chin and turning to the police chief. "Get him out of here, will you, Hollis? I've got 200 crab cakes and a couple of cases of champagne to attend to. Do come back after you've thrown him in whatever hole you can find. I'll save the good stuff for you."

Hollis blushed, then shoved Edwin down the ladder.

AFTER HOLLIS ARRESTED Edwin and fished Anton out of the water, the Coast Guard came and tugged the boat back to the dock. I found Beverlee sitting on a chair near the wedding arbor, her arms curled around her stomach, and a faraway look in her eyes. Matilda sat quietly in the cage at her feet.

I sat down next to her, wrapping my arm around her. "How are you holding up?"

She leaned her head against my shoulder and continued to stare out over the water. "I thought he was the one," she said quietly, a subdued smile barely lifting the corners of her mouth. "I wanted him to be the one."

With a sad smile, I gave her a gentle squeeze. "I wanted him to be the one, too."

Beverlee wiped a tear off her cheek with the hem of her velvet bustier. "I'm not sure what to do now."

"Let me get all these people squared away and I'll take you and Matilda home."

I picked up Matilda's cage and had started walking toward the dock when I heard Beverlee's voice from behind me. "What if I don't want to go home?" she asked.

I spun around and pasted on a determined smile. "We can go anywhere you want."

She stood and brushed off the front of her pirate gown, straightened her spine, then stopped in front of me. "I want to go to my party. I have enough crab cakes for an army and head-butting my groom at the altar made me hungry."

She brushed by me on her way to the dock, turning to lift a single finger. "But first we need to find you some pants," she said with a wink.

26

Beverlee's wedding guests didn't mention the absent groom. Instead, they eagerly accepted her plates of food and glasses of wine like they were at a pirate-themed costume party. She spent the evening being fussed over, her favorite thing, and more than once I sought her out in the crowd and found her smiling.

Scoots found me a pair of dark gray sweatpants and tennis shoes from the gym bag in her trunk. "No worries, they're clean," she said, and motioned down her body. "Does this look like the body of a woman who dirties her own athletic wear?"

The sky had gotten darker as the sun disappeared below the horizon. Beach music and laughter from the party drowned out the sounds of the water.

I had just stepped away from the reception tent to check on the catering truck when Ian stepped out of the shadows. He was heart-stoppingly handsome in a loose-fitting white linen shirt and khaki trousers. "Wild night," he said, his low voice rumbling against my ear. "But Beverlee seems to be handling it well."

I shrugged. "She loves a good get-together."

He scanned the reception, one side of his mouth turning up in a wry smile. "She and Scoots have formed a conga line."

I saw the two leading a string of women around the tent. They were all grinning and moving their bodies in tune with the music. "She'll be okay. Tomorrow will be harder than tonight, though. When she wakes up alone, she'll realize how much she lost."

"But she won't wake up alone. You'll be there."

I sighed. "For another few days, yes. But then I have to go back home." I had to deal with the threat of getting evicted and finding a job and hunting down the man who broke my heart and stole my money.

"That's right. You don't stay, do you?" His voice held an undercurrent of bitterness.

If felt like a punch to the stomach. But before I could respond, Ian spotted Hollis getting out of his patrol car nearby. He walked away without a backward glance.

Suddenly, I felt a nudge and the brush of cold, wet fur as Rusty, still damp from his dive into the water, leaned into my leg. I couldn't help but grin. "You saved my life earlier. Should we find you a reward?"

He trailed behind me, tail wagging, as I followed Hollis into the party tent in search of an errant dog biscuit or gold-plated bowl of steak.

Beverlee immediately greeted us with plates piled high with food. "You must be hungry," she gushed.

Rusty accepted a chunk of cornbread, wolfing it down in a single bite before rolling onto his back to wiggle in the grass.

Hollis moaned his approval as he popped a boiled shrimp into his mouth. "I've got to get back to the station, but I wanted to come out here to check on you." He lowered his voice and leaned in toward Beverlee. "You've had a long day."

Sadness flashed across her face for the briefest of moments before she reached out and patted him on the arm. "Don't you worry about me, Hollis Goodnight. I always land on my feet."

He cleared his throat and shoved in another bite of food. "He confesshed."

"What?" I said, leaning in to hear him better over the band, which had launched into a lively version of *My Girl*. "We couldn't understand you."

He wiped his mouth with a cocktail napkin and shook his head apologetically. "I'm sorry. I haven't eaten all day. What I was trying to say," he continued, "is that Anton confessed. Threw Edwin under the bus in exchange for our assurances we'd share his full cooperation with the judge. Turns out they've been using Doris's wedding planning business for more than happily ever afters. Those exotic tropical weddings she liked to brag about? Most of them were also exotic tropical smuggling operations."

He pulled the last piece of steak off a skewer and used the tiny sword to point to Beverlee. "And you were right at the center of it."

"Me?" She put a hand to her chest. "Hollis, I can assure you I had nothing to do with—"

He put his hand out to stop her. "I know you didn't. Not intentionally, at least." He swallowed, his face softening. "He was using you, Beverlee. I'm sorry."

Edwin's local fish market turned out to be the front for a small-scale money laundering outfit that involved moving diamonds into the United States and funneling them back out to serve as cash flow for a cartel out of the islands.

"The Bahamas?" Beverlee asked, wide-eyed. "We were supposed to fly to the Bahamas for our honeymoon tomorrow. He wanted me to bring along samples of some of my new line. He told me the Bahamian people really love Southern food and that there's a huge untapped market for—"

She realized what she was saying. "Ohhhh," she said, drawing the word out for several seconds.

Hollis nodded. "Those packages of cornbread mix you found were the prototypes. A false bottom was cut into each of them, supposedly to hold the diamonds in place so they wouldn't raise suspicion when you carried them across the border. They were planning on rebranding them with the new labels they designed for you. They were using your reputation, your celebrity, to be the face of their criminal activities."

"When I carried them across?" She huffed. "Do I look like a mule to you?"

We all shook our heads.

"No, of course not," I said, turning to Hollis. "But that still doesn't explain Doris. Or Bill."

"As you figured out earlier, Doris was Edwin's ex-wife. She was an artist, but she also had a knack for planning parties. She handled the weddings, and Edwin and Anton ran the behind-the-scenes." Hollis licked tartar sauce off his finger. "They targeted you, Beverlee. They had been planning this long before you and Edwin got together."

"The night she died," he continued, "Doris decided she wasn't so fond of being Edwin's ex. She wanted him back. She didn't like how real things seemed between you and Edwin, so she threatened to call the whole thing off."

My stomach dropped. "So, Edwin killed her. And then killed Old Bill because he figured it out, too."

Hollis shook his head. "Bill doesn't get off the hook that easily. He was involved in this, too. The warehouse building they used near the water? It belonged to him. Since the fishing business wasn't as lucrative as it used to be, he dabbled in crime to bring in more cash."

Scoots cleared her throat. "Not a good way to get a post office named after you, if you ask me."

I blinked several times, pieces of the puzzle finally falling into place. If Bill's warehouse was being used for the diamond smuggling, that explained why Dex had a copy of his property tax records. But it still didn't explain why Bill Judson had been murdered. "Then why did he...?"

Hollis motioned to Beverlee, whose face had turned white. "Turns out Bill had a soft spot for Beverlee. He couldn't go through with it. The text he sent you that night wasn't about meeting you to talk about the boat. He planned to warn you. Unfortunately, Edwin figured it out and killed him before he had a chance to spill the beans."

"He was trying to help me? But I thought Maggie..."

"Wasn't involved," Hollis said, shaking his head. "We found maps and diagrams of both crime scenes in her apartment, as well as a handful of raw diamonds we thought were part of the goods trafficking operation. And she was quick to confess."

Beverlee gasped. "She confessed to killing those people? Why would she do that if she was innocent?"

Hollis brushed her off with a wave. "It was all a big misunderstanding. She was trying to piece the puzzle together herself because Doris had been blackmailing her."

"For what?" Beverlee asked.

"For dipping her pink-polished big toe into somebody else's pool," I muttered under my breath.

"Magnolia and her boyfriend had found a stash of Edwin's diamonds in Doris's office and were close to putting the pieces together when Doris found out about their secret affair," Hollis said. "Doris was planning to use the pictures to bribe Dex after the election."

I nodded. "It never hurts to have a senator in your pocket when you're knee-deep in a smuggling operation. But that still doesn't explain why Maggie confessed."

"That was just a simple love story. She thought Dex killed Doris to protect her, so she confessed to the murder first to keep suspicion away from him."

Scoots plucked a meatball from Hollis's plate and pointed it toward Beverlee. "See, I told you. Relationships are nothing but trouble."

27

I stopped by Trolls the next day to say goodbye to Ian before I headed back to Raleigh.

His face was impassive as he told me his sister was moving into the apartment above the pawnshop until she figured out what to do without her fiancé.

"It turns out she knew," he said. "She knew Dex was cheating on her the whole time, but she was so far gone in process of planning their wedding to cancel it and let everyone down."

I nodded. "I can understand that. It's hard to be a failure when it feels like the whole world is watching."

Several seconds passed before he responded. "Nobody has ever thought of you as a failure, Glory. Wild and impulsive, yes. But not a failure. You taught this town how to have a good time."

I swallowed. Somewhere along the way, I had lost that girl. It was time to find her again.

And then he stepped forward and wrapped me in a tight hug. "It was good to see you. Stop by if you're ever in town again."

No passionate kiss. No begging me to stay. Not even a flash of dimple.

He just let me walk away. Just like he did the first time.

I SPENT my last few hours in Flat Falls helping Beverlee get rid of any evidence that Edwin ever existed in her life. She bought new sheets, started a bonfire with a pair of gabardine pants he'd left on the bathroom floor, and baked an enormous chocolate cake she hand-delivered to the county jail.

"He's lactose intolerant, so I used extra milk. Bless his heart," she said with a drawl. "I hope it gives him diarrhea."

I wiped a tear from my cheek as I hugged her goodbye. This woman had loved me when there was no reason to, and I could never repay her for that. "I love you, Beverlee," I whispered.

She ran her hand down my hair, then stopped to pat my cheek. "I love you, too, baby girl."

I vowed to myself that I'd make her proud.

I promised to visit more often, a vow I repeated when I stopped by to say goodbye to Josie before I rolled my suitcase out to the waiting car.

"You can't leave just when things between you and Ian are getting steamy again," she said with a punch to my arm.

"I went by to see him earlier. Believe me, he's not interested in heating things up with me again."

"His loss," Josie said with a sad smile.

I waved back over my shoulder as I headed down the stairs one last time. "Stay out of trouble."

She chuckled as she shut the door behind me.

I glanced back up at the apartment, then across at Ian's boat. I thought when the time came for me to head out of

Flat Falls again, I would do so with a big grin and a backward wave, like I did the last time I left.

Instead, I felt... heavy. Everything from my feet to my brain was bogged down with the weight of these farewells.

I wheeled the suitcase to the trunk and popped it open. I bent over to pick it up and came face-to-face with a cold, wet nose.

"Rusty, you scared me." I ran my hand along his back, a knot forming in my throat.

He plunked down on the ground at my feet, and I leaned in for one final cuddle. His fur was warm from the sun, and he smelled like freshly cut grass and corn chips, and I wished I could bottle him up to pull out every time I needed a boost.

I gave him a soft kiss on his forehead. "Be good."

He hopped to his feet and stepped over to my trunk, tail wagging. He bent over and dropped his favorite yellow tennis ball on top of my suitcase, then sat back down.

I laughed. "Nice try, but I can't play right now." I picked up the ball and dropped it on the ground next to him, wiping my hand off on my pants. "Gross."

Rusty looked at me, then the ball. He picked it up and dropped it on top of my bag again.

A tear slid down my cheek and I sank to the ground next to him. "I'll miss you, too, you big, stinky goof."

Then I climbed in the Honda and headed home.

THERE WAS VERY little fanfare when I notified my landlord of my plans to vacate the house because I wasn't able to afford the rent anymore. He simply nodded and patted my arm, then ushered me out the door with promises to help me with anything I might need as I moved on to the next phase of my life.

I folded the newspaper where I had circled a few apartments that looked like they might fall on the cheap-but-not-filled-with-mice-droppings side and tucked it into my purse.

The air seemed fresher when I stepped onto the front porch, my hands filled with trash bags containing the remnants of my life with Cobb. Sprinklers clicked gently in the distance, and dogs barked their good morning hellos to the world. A young woman in jogging pants waved as she pushed a stroller down the street. Life showed every intention of moving on. It was time for me to do the same.

The weight on my shoulders lifted with each bag I carried out and gently tossed to the curb. I took a deep breath and glanced around. It wasn't every day you said goodbye to the life you thought you knew.

I went back inside to wrestle with the sofa, the last piece of history I had to unload before I moved on. I had planned on calling Goodwill to pick it up, but I needed to get it out onto the front porch so I could lock up behind me on my way out.

Wooden furniture legs scraped across the floor as I shoved it toward the door. Eventually, through a series of well-executed squats and even more curses, I made it to the doorway. But no matter how hard I pushed, the sofa wouldn't move any farther. It was wedged in that door frame like a two-ton elephant in too-tight Spanx.

With a frustrated grunt, I closed my eyes and shoved one more time to loosen it.

"Good heavens, girl. You're about to give yourself a hemorrhoid."

I turned quickly to see Scoots, coffee cup in hand, standing at the bottom of my steps. I threw myself over the sofa and into her outstretched arms. "What are you doing here?"

"Came to help."

"How did you know I was here?"

"Beverlee. She knows everything. She called us a few days ago and said we should plan a road trip."

I craned my neck to check out the sidewalk behind her. "Us?"

Scoots nodded and held up her phone. "We FaceTimed in the criminal since the state of North Carolina has prohibited her from leaving her apartment." Josie gave a perky wave from the small screen.

I smiled and waved back. "It's so good to see you," I said, and it was true. I hadn't been gone from Flat Falls long, but I missed these people.

Scoots gestured down the street, where Beverlee was trying to parallel park. "She can't park worth a darn. You must have gotten that from her side of the family. I jumped out when I saw what you were doing so I could talk you out of it."

"Talk me out of what? Moving?"

"Oh no, it's time for that. I wanted to talk you out of trying to cram this ugly… and large… piece of furniture through that not-so-large hole." She gestured toward the door.

I smiled. "You're right. It's not going to fit, is it?"

Just then, Beverlee climbed up the porch steps and handed me a cup of steaming coffee. "Nice bags under your eyes. This should help."

Emotion welled up in my throat. "It's good to see you guys, but why are you here?"

Beverlee turned and cocked out a hip, pursing her lips. "We're here to bring you home."

I looked at her in confusion, my hand waving around the almost-empty house. "I *am* home, Beverlee."

"No, I mean home to Flat Falls."

My vision blurred as tears began to build. "Beverlee, you've been my only family for as long as I can remember. But you said it yourself. You need space, you need freedom. It's my fault you didn't get that."

She took my hand in hers and pulled me around to the front of the sofa. She settled next to me and pulled our clasped hands into her lap. "Oh, Glory, is that what you think? That you somehow held me back?"

I didn't trust myself to speak, so I nodded, a single tear sliding down my cheek and landing with a dark splat on the front of my T-shirt.

"It can't have been easy on you, losing your mama and daddy so young." She rubbed her thumb along my palm. "But there isn't a moment since that day that I would change. Welcoming you into my home is the best thing I've ever done. And I couldn't have asked for a better daughter."

I choked back a sob. "I have no idea where to go from here. Everything is… broken."

Scoots stepped forward and slapped me on the back, coffee sloshing out of her paper cup and onto the floor. "Rock bottom's not a bad place to be, kiddo. It's a great place to start your next adventure."

"It would be too awkward," I said, shaking my head. "I don't think some people would welcome me back to town with a parade."

Scoots grunted. "Then some people need to mind their own business."

I wiped my eyes with the back of my sleeve. "I was actually thinking of one particular person."

"Who, Ian?" Her brow furrowed. "It wouldn't be too hard to hide his body. I know people."

I had been trying to avoid thoughts of Ian's body for a week. I smiled. "Despite how it ended, that would be a shame. It's a pretty good body. It would be a disservice to the world, like throwing out a Picasso."

I heard Josie's voice coming from the phone's speaker. I focused on the screen, and she raised her water bottle in a toast. "Amen to that."

"Hollis asked me to give this to you." Beverlee reached into her tote bag and pulled out an envelope. "He said you'd understand what it was. He also said to call him if you need backup with it."

I studied the envelope. There were no markings. It was smooth and white. I slid my finger under the flap and popped open the seal. I pulled out a single piece of paper. An address in Virginia, written in Hollis's neat, blocky hand-writing.

Hollis had found my ex-husband.

A zip of power shot through me. It was about time for Cobb to come face-to-face with what he had done. I might have let him walk all over me during our marriage, but I was still a Wells. Wells women could do very few things better than turn a simple grudge into an all-out war.

I folded the paper up and gently slid it back into the envelope. "Tell Hollis thank you for me."

Beverlee shook her head. "You can tell him yourself when you come back home. And besides, we've already picked out an office space for you."

"What kind of office space?" I asked. "I don't even have a business."

Scoots walked over and sat on the other side of me. "There's a vacant space on the other side of the pawnshop. It's yours if you want it."

"We've already got your business cards printed. You can't say no when it's on paper." Beverlee dipped her hand back into her bag, emerging with a stack of glossy red cards. My name was embossed in silver on the front, along with the name Carolina Weddings.

I chuckled and shook my head. "I'm not a wedding planner, Beverlee. I think we established that last week. And you can't have a wedding planner that doesn't believe in happily ever after, can you? All that lace. All that white. All that love." I shuddered.

Her lips turned up slightly. "Everybody deserves love, baby. Even those of us who have been down the aisle a time or two."

"Or four," Scoots said with a snort from across the room, where she leaned against the fireplace and held up her phone so Josie could see everything.

"Or four," Beverlee smiled. "That's what's going to make you good at it. You'll be the wedding planner for those of us with unconventional stories or checkered romantic histories. The only way a broken heart can heal is to love again… and again… and again. Scuffed-up love is still worth celebrating."

"Isn't there already a wedding planner in Flat Falls?"

Beverlee dismissed me with a wave. "Who, Magnolia? Yeah, she's taking over for Doris. But she's got her hands full with all those typical brides with their church bells and white fondant and ten-foot-long trains. And, frankly, she needs a little competition."

I studied the card. "A wedding planner for renegade and offbeat brides?"

Beverly nodded, her hair bouncing and a rosiness in her cheeks I hadn't seen since before the fiasco with Edwin. "And we'll all be there to help you."

I ran away from Flat Falls the first time because I was afraid my life would be too small there and that I would never escape the things that had shaped me. But it turns out that life grows in direct proportion to the energy you put into it. And despite the dead bodies and the judgmental neighbors, being back in Flat Falls had made me feel alive again.

I took one last look around the house that held my dreams in what seemed like another lifetime. Things had changed since then. I was now unemployed and homeless, and there weren't any ties keeping me here. The only ties I had were those I chose.

I took a deep breath before I turned to Beverlee and Scoots with a grin. "Okay, I'm in."

A spark of excitement flashed in my belly. A new start in an old place, with people who knew my history and loved me, anyway. With a family who chose me, again and again.

Home.

THE END

ACKNOWLEDGMENTS

Many thanks to the fantastic team of people who helped bring this book to life. While writing is often a solitary endeavor, publishing certainly isn't, and I am so grateful for the expertise and enthusiasm of the people by my side.

Special thanks to Mariah Sinclair for the design that started it all. To Stacy Juba, Beth Hale, Michelle Benningfield, and the team at Victory Editing, please accept my sincere gratitude for helping making the story stronger.

To the authors who have inspired me and those who walk this road with me, you rock. Many thanks to Liz Tully and the supportive women in Secondary Characters, Becca Syme, and Carrie Ann Ryan for helping me keep my head on straight and being so generous with your pep talks.

Thank you to my agent, Jana Hanson, for your tireless efforts to bring Glory's story to the world.

To all the friends and family who cheered me on along the way, I could not have done this without your support. Diane and Kathy, thank you for stepping in with high-fives and childcare when my sanity was wearing thin. Karen

Brock, you have encouraged me more times than I can count, and I am so thankful for your friendship and support.

Mom and Dad, to say you were my earliest readers does you an injustice. You've read everything I wrote since I was a pre-teen writing angsty poetry in a spiral notebook. Thank you for your unwavering belief in me and my stories.

Finally, I offer a wholehearted thank you to my husband Sean and our three sweet kiddos. You cheered for me, with actual applause, when I felt stuck. You brought me coffee and left me love notes. You believed in me, and I am the luckiest woman alive because I get to spend my days with you.

ABOUT THE AUTHOR

Erin Scoggins is a long-time Southerner with a fondness for offbeat humor and pickled okra. After fifteen years in marketing with a Fortune 500 company, she traded her MBA for fictional crime scenes and small-town scandals. She writes fun, flirty mysteries that are celebrations of food, family, and the killer South.

Craving something tasty? Nothing beats Beverlee's famous Bless Your Heart Cake.

Visit Erin at www.ErinScoggins.com/cookbook to get your free copy of *'Til Death Do Us Dine*, a collection of Southern snacks, sips, sweets, and stories to help you slay your next celebration.